Daniel & Erik's Super Fab Ultimate Wedding Checklist

Daniel & Erik's Super Fab Ultimate Wedding Checklist

K.E. BELLEDONNE

interlude press • new york

interlude ✦ press • new york

To S, always.
Ever yours, ever mine, ever ours.
Thank you for agreeing to never, ever get married again.

"Beetroot chips are an abomination." In his friend Kate's tiny apartment kitchen, Daniel poured the chips into a bowl.

"Danny, please," Kate wheedled over the sound of the party, smoothing her brown hair. "Please just go talk to him, okay? He came with Antonio and that bitch Annika, and now he's just standing there. This is our third date; I need things to go well with Antonio tonight, okay? You know how badly I need to get laid. Please, Danny. Just go talk to him for a few minutes."

"Who the hell likes beetroot chips, anyway?" Daniel muttered, frowning at the bowl of vegetable chips on the counter in front of him.

"Oh, my god. Stop complaining." Kate slammed a platter of cheese and crackers on the counter before unwrapping the cellophane from it. "You've been complaining about the chips since you got here."

"What's wrong with Doritos? Everyone likes Doritos."

"Nothing, if you're twelve-year-old boy. They are the number one snack choice of twelve-year-old boys. This is not a party for twelve-year-old boys, so we're not having them."

"I'm just saying, some non-hipster food would be nice."

"Oh, for Christ's sakes, enough with the complaining. Go talk to the cute boy."

"Which one is he, again?" Daniel tried to peer nonchalantly out of the kitchen and surveyed the crowd of people.

"The one over near Antonio, with the dark hair." Kate joined him at the kitchen door, craning her neck. "Well, he *was* near Antonio. Oh, my god, he's the one on the couch, *reading a book.* Who reads a book at a party?"

"Someone either horrifically bored or not from this country."

"Daaaaa-niel!" Kate whined.

"Kaaaaaate," Daniel replied, rolling his eyes at her irritation.

She slapped his arm. "You are going to drive me to drink."

"You're going to drink anyway."

"True." She stuck her tongue out at him and shoved the bowl of chips into his hands. "Now, go be nice."

"I'm always nice."

"Fuck you, you are not. Danny, just go talk to him. A few minutes, that's all I'm asking."

"I hate you."

"You do not, and we both know it." She smirked. "Just keep him entertained long enough for Antonio to *not* have to feel obligated to leave. Come on, the poor guy's only been working with Antonio at the university for a couple of weeks. He doesn't really know anyone. He's so far from home, and it's Christmas, for god's sake."

"Turning him into a sob story does not make me any more enthused to go make awkward small talk with a complete stranger. Does he even speak English?"

"You are such a snob and a giant pain in my ass. Yes, he speaks English. His name is Erik. Antonio says he's a great guy. *And* he's gay."

"Oh, for fuck's sake, that is not an automatic thing. Just because he's gay doesn't mean that he can't also be an absolute ass. They are not mutually exclusive things."

"Danny," she whined.

"You owe me, Kiki Dee. You owe me."

Daniel threaded his way through Kate's tiny open-plan apartment, dodging groups and clumps of people laughing and chatting and nearly having to shout over the music pouring from the stereo speakers. A holiday party was in full swing; here and there people wore brightly colored felted reindeer antlers or elf ears, and no one seemed to mind. The beer and wine flowed freely, and everyone seemed to be having a good time.

It was a good party, Daniel decided. The guests included several friends he hadn't seen in a while and a bunch of people he didn't know. He noticed several promising young men, prospective dates and mutually accepted one-night stands. It had been a while since he'd broken up with Matthew for the final time, and he felt good and stable after such a long time of feeling shaky. He was definitely looking for easy—nothing serious, no strings. He intended to relish being single for a while, to take his time on the dating scene.

And he was definitely going to take his time with that gorgeous blond guy from Kate's work in the corner, once he fulfilled his promise to go talk to Erik, Nordic archaeologist and apparently world's most awkward party-goer.

Engrossed in flipping through a coffee table book, Erik sat at the end of Kate's brown leather couch. He wore corduroys and a blue and green checked shirt with the sleeves rolled up almost to his elbows to show off muscled forearms that still hadn't lost their summer suntan. Daniel wiped his palms on his jeans as he got closer.

"Hi," Daniel said.

A shock of brown hair flopped as Erik glanced up from his reading. His dark brown eyes looked Daniel over. "Hello."

Then the bastard went back to reading as if Daniel wasn't even there.

"Um, okay," Daniel said. He knew if he gave up, Kate would probably castrate him. He could feel her eyes on him from across the room, where she was chatting with someone who must be Antonio. At least, Daniel hoped it was Antonio because her level of flirtation was ridiculous—flashing a smile, playing with her hair. Meeting a guy like Antonio—admittedly, gorgeous and intelligent—in a coffee shop was just too perfect, and she seemed determined to make it work out.

Daniel smiled apologetically at Erik, who wasn't looking at him anyway. He perched on the arm of the couch next to him. "Hey, sorry to bother you, but my friend is going to kill me if I don't appear to be talking to you for at least a few minutes."

Erik looked up from the book and smiled with one eyebrow quirked up. "I'm sorry?"

"My friend, Kate, over there." Daniel nodded his head in her general direction. "She—look, she really likes your friend Antonio, and she wanted me to come over here and chat with you for a little bit and make sure you were doing okay, so maybe Antonio wouldn't feel like he had to leave the party early and—"

"Ah." Erik scratched his head. "Okay."

"So, hi."

"Hi," Erik said, smiling briefly.

"I'm Daniel. Daniel Whitcomb."

"Erik Kappel." He nodded.

"And Kate says you're an archaeologist?"

"Yes. Well, I'm an *anthropologist*. Mainly studying patterns of habitation and agriculturalization in Gotland at the end of the Vendel Period."

Daniel chuckled. "I'm sorry, I have no idea what that is."

"Vikings. In their homes." Erik smiled. "It's a little more complicated than that, but—"

"That's cool." Daniel fiddled with the seam of the couch. "The only thing I know about Vikings is from that TV show."

"It's not a *terrible* show." Erik looked down at the book again.

Trying to think of something else to say, Daniel glanced around the room. "So, ummm—"

"Did you know that Meyer lemons are thought to be a cross between a regular lemon and a mandarin orange?" Erik said.

"I beg your pardon?"

Erik held up the book he'd been reading as evidence. "Meyer lemons."

"Ah," Daniel smiled. So, this guy might a little weird, but he was trying to keep the conversation going. *Weird and kind of adorable.*

"And almost the entire crop of Meyer lemon trees in the US had to be destroyed in the 1940s because it was found they carried a virus that killed off other citrus trees?"

"The book says that, too?"

"Yes." Erik smiled as he looked down and smoothed the pages.

"Hey, move over," Daniel said as he nudged at Erik's knee. He grinned widely when Erik slid over, leaving enough room for Daniel to slide off the arm of the couch and sit next to him.

They spent the next few minutes looking at the coffee table book about lemons, pointing out interesting things in the glossy photographs or just smiling as Erik slowly flipped the pages of the book. As they neared the last page, Daniel got up to get them each another beer. He came back quickly, ignoring Kate's raised and knowing eyebrows as he walked by her.

Daniel sat next to Erik and handed him his beer. "So, uhhh." Daniel took a nervous sip of his beer. "What's Gotland?"

Erik's eyes lit up with excitement as he began explaining the area of Sweden on which his research focused. Daniel's stomach flip-flopped. *This guy is actually really good-looking,* he thought. Erik's brown eyes sparkled, and Daniel tried very hard not to be distracted from what he was saying. He had no idea eyes actually could sparkle—that was bullshit from movies and books, wasn't it?

After Erik finished his explanation, Daniel took another swig of beer. "You know, I'd always kind of assumed that Vikings were from Norway, not Sweden. I don't know why I had that idea, but—"

"At that time, there weren't countries known as 'Norway' or 'Sweden,'" Erik explained. "It's all one big landmass, you know. I mean, there's probably research into why people assume Vikings are from Norway, but I don't know who's doing it."

"Maybe Norway just has better marketing," Daniel said as he swirled the last of his beer.

"Better marketing," Erik said softly, then chuckled and shook his head. "That's a good one."

Daniel stared into his beer bottle, searching for a good topic of conversation. This was the first time he'd felt pleasantly awkward around a guy in a very long time, in that slightly sheepish and bubbling hopeful sort of way. He wanted to keep talking to him, wanted to keep that feeling going.

"Here's a question I've always wondered about: Do archaeologists really use paintbrushes to brush dirt away from things, like Indiana Jones?"

Erik smiled brightly. Goddammit, Daniel was done for. The way Erik's eyes seemed to come alive when he explained something; the way his head dipped to the side when he was trying to remember a word; the way his hands moved as he talked. Daniel was just done for.

"Actually," Erik began, "there's a thing next week about excavation techniques, if you're interested."

Daniel paused. "Yeah. Yeah, that sounds cool."

"Ok, good." Erik caught someone's eye over Daniel's shoulder and frowned. He stood up abruptly. "Here's my number. The class begins at eleven. Sorry, Annika is ready to leave. I have to go."

"So are you going to see him again?" Kate asked as they finished washing the dishes after the party.

"Who?"

"Oh, for fuck's sake, Danny. The gorgeous Swedish archaeologist—"

"He was born here and grew up in Germany. He *studies* Sweden. And he's an *anthropologist*."

"Whatever." She flicked soap suds at him. "Are you going to see him again?"

"I mean, he gave me major flirtation vibes. And he gave me his number. But then he bolted as soon as Annika—"

"—that bitch," Kate interrupted. "Go on."

"Whatever. I don't know her. As soon as she, like, snapped her fingers, he was up and out of there."

"I don't know, Danny." Kate struggled with rinsing a large mixing bowl in her small sink. "He was giving you major goo-goo eyes while you guys were talking."

"I'm not interested in going out with someone who jumps whenever some chick says boo."

"Particularly that chick. She and Antonio and Erik passed their written exams last semester and are all just working on their thesis research and teaching." Kate said. She worked as the anthropology department's administrative assistant. "She's a nightmare in staff meetings. She is seriously one of the most unpleasant people I've ever had to be around. She's just a bitch, all the time."

Daniel paused. "I don't know. I got a really—a really good feeling about him. And he did invite me to something next week, I think."

"You think?"

"But, not like a serious thing. Like, a class. I think."

"So, what's the deal with him?"

Daniel bent to put a cutting board away in a low cabinet. "He's... he's cool. He's weird. He was really easy to talk to, once we got going. He's easy to be around. It was nice. I mean, it was a really strange way to leave the party, but before that, it was really nice."

"You're welcome."

"Oh, fuck off. So, I got to sit next to a nice guy for a few minutes while you tried to hook up with his friend and I'm supposed to thank you?"

"It's just been so long—"

"Since you got laid? Shut up, there was that waiter, like, last month."

"No, dummy. Since *you've* been on a date, Danny. It's been forever—"

"It has not been forever, but thank you. And I don't think this counts as a date. Right now, it doesn't feel like a date."

"What does it feel like?"

Daniel let the water out of the sink. "It feels kind of weird and completely normal and pedestrian and not like a date."

TEN MONTHS BEFORE THE WEDDING

GOOD MORNING, DANIEL!

Welcome to Aurora, your digital life planner!

Thank you for choosing our Ultimate Wedding Planning App! We know planning your wedding can be an overwhelming task—let Aurora keep you organized! Click <u>here</u> to take your guided tour of Aurora's planning capabilities. Collect and coordinate photos, videos and MP4s of vendors, caterers, bands and more! Merge messages and sync calendars with your wedding party! Use our partner site, BeStabulous, to post photos of everything from reception ideas to honeymoon destinations. Get invitees involved in your planning with polls, comment threads and ranking capabilities! Why just pin something when you can stab it? BeStabulous is the world's most fabulous idea-gathering website, especially for the world's most fabulous people.

☑ Personalize, materialize and actualize! With Aurora, you can do it all!

You've got a lot of decisions to make, so let's get cracking!

Here is your to-do list for today:

☑ *Choose your date! (Click <u>here</u> for calendar.)*

☑ *Pick your wedding party (Click <u>here</u> to forward Aurora to your specified email distribution list.)*

☑ *Research photographers, bands, florists and caterers. (Click <u>here</u> to enter vendor information in your address book. Click <u>here</u> to save vendor contracts. Click <u>here</u> to enter your photo gallery.)*

☑ *Start the guest list. (Click <u>here</u> to import all contacts. Some social media sites may require additional authorization.)*

☑ *Work out your budget. (Click <u>here</u> for spreadsheet.)*

☑ *Reserve your date and venue. (Click <u>here</u> for calendar.)*

☑ *Book your officiant. (Click <u>here</u> to enter officiant information to your address book. Click <u>here</u> to enter officiant contract.)*

☑ *Click here to add or modify list entries. Showing 1-6 out of 70 checklist entries left to complete.*

What's trending on Aurora? How To Find The Right Yodeler For Your Alpine-themed Wedding! Click <u>here</u> to read the article about your next wedding must-have!

Have a great day, Daniel!

Happy Planning!
Aurora

**

Click on checkboxes to mark task as complete, or on task name to edit/modify.
Unsubscribe from reminders.
Use Aurora to keep you organized while planning life's big events or simply the big
event of life. Check out our suite of sister apps with fully customizable planning
capabilities!

📱

DANIEL FROWNED AT THE APP on his phone. He and Erik had only been engaged forty-eight hours and yet somehow he was already way behind in planning their wedding.

"—and he'd like to have the Bucket of Spuds, as usual." Erik ordered for Daniel at their usual brunch spot. Daniel always got the same thing, despite always wondering aloud about ordering something different, every time. "No sour cream and add some extra avocado, please."

"And how would he like his egg?"

"Over easy." Erik smiled at her.

The waitress jotted a note on her pad, took both menus from Erik and smiled. "I'll be right back with some more coffee."

"Thank you, Amelia." Erik watched her flit away before turning his attention to Daniel. "What's this?"

"We're really behind on this wedding planning thing. I just put in a random date in June." Daniel chewed his lip. "I mean, I knew there was a lot of planning to be done, but this is—"

"Well, what's first on the list? Let's be methodical about this."

"Pick your date."

"Hmmm." Erik rubbed his nose. "June's a good month? What about the twenty-second?"

"Is that even a weekend?"

"No idea." Erik sounded unconcerned. "We can worry about that later. What's next?"

"Pick your wedding party."

"Simple. No wedding party. Done. And next?"

"No wedding party? Are you serious? We've been together three years, and sometimes I still can't tell when you're joking."

"Yes. Why do we need these people?"

"Because..." Daniel knew there was a good reason to have a wedding party. He knew there was. He envisioned a wedding party, with coordinating shoes and bow ties—maybe cravats? Or maybe the men could wear morning suits with lavender accents. Was a top hat too much?

"Daniel? Do we need these people?"

"Yes. We do. I mean—" he paused again. "The wedding party is supposed to be people who mean a lot to us, who've helped us, who support us and will continue to support us in our marriage."

"And they are completely necessary?"

"Well, I don't know about 'necessary.'" Daniel frowned at his silverware, trying to figure out how to explain what he meant. "I know there are several people I would really love to have standing up there with me, as like a—like a formal acknowledgment of how much I care about them."

"But you could just tell them this? How much you care about them?"

"Yes, but... It's not quite the same."

"This means a great deal to you, yes?" Erik said softly. "To have these special people there to witness our wedding day?"

"Yes."

"Then we'll figure out how to make it happen."

Daniel took a sip of the dregs of his coffee. "I was thinking we could have three people, each? Maybe four?"

"Four? For each of us?"

"Well, to have balance. I mean, it would look better when we're all standing up at the front and in the photos and things like that. Although, I suppose, it kind of depends on the venue. If it's too small, then eight people in the wedding party will just look ridiculous."

"So, let's choose a venue." Erik took Daniel's hand and rubbed it.

"We need a date, first."

"I bet we need to start with a budget first. Everything always depends on the budget," Erik said gloomily. Archaeology was a fascinating, but not a lucrative, profession. "Every study, every excavation, nothing goes forward without a budget."

Amelia returned with their coffee. Daniel poured milk into his and took a sip. He shuddered.

"You forgot the sugar," Erik said. "You always put sugar in the coffee here."

"Well, but at some places, the coffee is already weirdly sweet, so if you add the sugar before you try it, it just winds up being disgusting."

"Yes, but *here*, you always put the sugar in."

Daniel ripped open the sugar packet, stirred it in and chewed his lip again as he scrolled through the rest of the checklist.

"Oh, my fucking god, there are seventy entries already and at least seventeen other checklists." He drank his coffee. "Look here, oh my god. 'Shoe-buying checklist.' 'Honeymoon packing checklist.' 'Engagement party planning checklist.' At least that one only has seven entries."

"Engagement party! Let's start planning that!"

"We can't plan the engagement party until we know who's going to be on the guest list for the wedding. It's just tacky to invite people to the engagement party if they won't be invited to the wedding."

"But if they're going to be the exact same people there to support us and celebrate us getting married, then why do we need to do it twice? Let's just do the engagement party checklist, invite everyone we love, have a great party and call it good."

Daniel scoffed. "We just can't do that. That's just not how—that's just not how it's done."

"But, why not?" Erik blew on his coffee.

"Because, it's just not. I don't know how they do weddings in Germany or Sweden or wherever, but—"

"There are ridiculous people having ridiculous, overblown weddings all over the planet."

"I've been to a *ton* of them here. I know how this goes. There's a lot of weird rules that need to be followed—"

"Rules? Who made them?"

"Who made them? What do you mean who made them? The—everyone. Everyone made them. There are just certain things that happen at weddings, and they've always been that way and that's just the way—that's the way weddings go. Haven't you ever thought about how your wedding would go?"

"Not recently, no." Erik smiled.

"Well, I have. I've been thinking about weddings since I was eight years old, when I planned my first wedding—to Jo from *The Facts of Life.*"

"Which one was that?" Erik's grasp of American popular culture sometimes had distressing blanks, in Daniel's opinion.

"Oh, the tomboy. A real tough girl. Not girly at all."

"Why I am not surprised?" Erik said, wryly.

Daniel chuckled. "Yes, well, looking back, I suppose that might have been a clue."

"You've been dreaming of your perfect wedding since you were eight years old?" His eyes soft, Erik gazed at him. "You're such a romantic."

"I mean, not continuously or anything," Daniel muttered. Erik's intensity still unnerved him at times.

"Then we need to do what we can to make *this* your dream wedding. You're only getting married once, *to me*, and we won't get a second chance at it."

Daniel's throat closed up a little; he was overwhelmed by Erik's insistence that Daniel's dreams, no matter how small, were important and worth pursuing.

"You know what is not on this checklist?" Daniel beamed, taking his hand. "Purchasing your fiancé's engagement ring, and I would very much like to talk about that one."

Daniel tucked his feet up on the diner booth's bench and curled into Erik's side, gooey-eyed and adoring. Erik let out what might, from another man, be described as a "giggle."

Several hours later, Erik squinted at the notes he'd scribbled on the paper placemat. Brunch had been full of wedding plans and ideas, some agreed-upon, some debated hotly.

"So, my part of the wedding party will be Antonio and Annika—"

"Annika will look gorgeous in lavender, even if she is a vampire bitch, but I'm not sure Antonio's coloring will work with purples," Daniel murmured, making notes on his own placemat.

"Let's not get distracted, love. And be nice about Annika."

"Right. Okay, so you get Antonio and Kirsten, and I'm going to have Kate and..."

Erik raised his eyebrows expectantly.

"Kate and I don't know who, yet. I need to think about it some more. I mean, if we're only having two attendants, I need to do a lot of narrowing down." Daniel chewed on his lip. Of his four co-creators at Co-Op—Stasia, who knit; Andre, who threw pottery; Carynne, who made her own jewelry; and Stefan, who mixed teas and baked—he couldn't say to whom he was closest. What with their creations, the location they'd lucked into and just the right price points, Co-Op had become the darling of the hipster set and quite a success. But deciding which of his co-owners would be in his wedding party would cause problems.

"We already decided two attendants was the right number: enough to be helpful and supportive, but not enough to be ridiculous."

"Okay, well, yes. I agree. I just don't know how I'm going to decide."

"Tell them you're choosing the one you love best." Erik grinned at the waitress refilling their coffee. "And then let them duke it out. First one to draw blood wins."

"Thanks, that's very helpful," Daniel muttered, slurping scalding hot coffee out of his mug. "You and your bloody Viking mind..."

THREE YEARS AGO

The brown sweater brought out his eyes, and the green sweater went well with his skin tone. Both sweaters, however, were a little tight this winter. Daniel could hear his ex, Matthew, insinuating, "If you want to stop jiggling like a walrus every winter, you should probably stop eating so many carbs."

That statement was technically true, and Daniel felt a twinge of guilt adding it to his list of Matthew's faults. There were ways to tell the truth that didn't sting so badly, though. Daniel snorted derisively as he pawed through his closet, looking for something else to wear. Matthew was demonstrably, and by the very definition, an asshole, and Daniel was lucky to be rid of him.

He chose a black V-neck, pilled and slightly faded. Warm and soft and oversized, it was one sweater he hadn't worn in public. He tossed it on over a white T-shirt, put on his one pair of jeans that didn't have ink or bleach spots and shoved his feet into his boots. He looked okay, he thought as he wound his scarf around his neck. Not great, not fancy, certainly not as if he was dressed up for a date. He could hear Matthew sneering and Kate's nagging chatter in his head and resisted the urge to go run put on something they'd consider "appropriate for a date." Something tight and uncomfortable and most likely itchy.

No. He was going to be comfortable, he was going to be himself, and if this guy didn't like him being comfortable, then screw him. Daniel wasn't going to shove himself into the clothes, the body, the personality

16

he thought some guy would like. This time around, he was going to be himself and no one else.

The wooden floors creaked as Daniel made his way across his small attic apartment. He knocked a brightly colored throw pillow on the floor as he grabbed his parka and scarf from the arm of his shabby couch. He clattered down the rickety stairs and flung open the side door to the shop.

The shop, Co-Op, was in an old rambling building right on Emerson Street West, the burgeoning and quickly gentrifying hipster area of Tallenburg. As in many New England college towns, retro tattoo artists, organic goat milk soap producers, custom artisan leatherworkers and a quasi-vintage bakery named Tasty Buns shared their block.

Daniel straightened price tags as he went quickly toward the back and realized it was probably time to take everything off the shelves and displays to dust again. He'd have to remember to get an extra bottle of glass cleaner and maybe some silver polish for the jewelry he and Carynne had been working on.

"Hello! Goodbye! I'm outta here!" He shouted toward the back room and to whomever was working today.

"What's the matter, you?" Stasia Pavlenko popped out of the small inventory closet. Short, round and fierce, with a personality as sharp as the spike she had pierced through one earlobe, she was one of Daniel's favorite people. There was no bullshit with Stasia. "You got a hot date or something?"

"As a matter of fact, I do." Daniel grinned sheepishly. "Or, a something, at least."

"Ooh! Get it, Danny!"

Daniel snorted. "It's ten a.m. on a Tuesday. I highly doubt there will be any 'getting it' going on."

"Well, you look nice," she said as she looped and tied his scarf around his neck. "I'm so glad you took this one. While I was knitting it, I was kind of freaked that someone would buy it who wouldn't appreciate it. It felt so good on the needles, you know?"

"I couldn't resist the yarn name, so appetizing—what was it, 'things rotting in a puddle outside the garbage depot?'"

"'Urban Decay,' jackass." She slapped at his chest. "Okay, go on now. Be yourself, stand up straight and don't forget to use a condom, even for oral."

"Ugh." He laughed. "You're awful."

"Yeah. I know. Now get the fuck out of here and have fun."

Twenty minutes later, Daniel stepped off the Front Street streetcar. He knew even if he walked slowly, ridiculously slowly, up Chatham Avenue, he would still arrive at Palmer Hall, Tallenburg University's sciences building, at least ten minutes early to meet Erik for their first meet-up/date/Daniel-didn't-know-what-to-call-it. It was a curse, afflicting him since he was kid—he was either incredibly, uncomfortably early for things or incredibly, absurdly late for them. Never on time.

He walked up the avenue, which was lined on both sides with stately trees with bare branches covered in ice. It had snowed the week before last; this was the first white Christmas Daniel could remember in years. A cold snap had set in soon afterward, leaving sharply jagged edges to the snow, which crunched as he walked. His thinly insulated hiking boots weren't meant for cold like this. His toes were still numb from the walk to the streetcar, and, despite his scarf, his ears were beginning to burn from the cold.

Daniel couldn't remember if they'd discussed *where* to meet at Palmer Hall. Was it at the main office? Or should he wait outside on the main steps? Would that seem too eager? Daniel slowly climbed the granite steps toward the front door. To get all nervous and worked up about where to meet was just silly, and he needed to relax about it.

He used his early arrival to take a quick look around the lobby. It was humid inside; the old marble walls and floors retained a chilly clamminess the fancy new heating system could do nothing about. He slipped slightly as he stepped onto the marble floor from the large entrance carpeting designed to catch the slush and snow from people's boots. He caught no sign of Erik in the crowds of students tromping up and down the steps going to and from class and went back outside.

Daniel blew out his breath in a long, slow cloud of white. It was a beautiful winter day, if bitterly cold; bright sunshine glinted off the snow. He leaned against the wrought iron railing of the steps and sniffed. He stamped his feet and shook his legs one at a time to keep the blood flowing, starting the ridiculous faux-nonchalant dance of someone waiting out in the cold.

He saw Erik coming out the front door of a building not far away, jogging down the front steps with a serious, almost determined look on his face. He wore a dark sweater with a thick rolled collar, no jacket, and his hair was disheveled—Daniel couldn't tell whether it was on purpose. Daniel pitied the undergrads in his classes, swooning every which way over the dark and serious soon-to-be-Dr. Kappel.

Head down as if studying his boots, Erik shoved his hands in his jeans pockets as he walked up the sidewalk. He glanced up, caught Daniel staring at him and smiled warmly as he sped up.

"You should have waited inside," he chided as he walked to Daniel. "It's cold out."

"Bah," Daniel disagreed, grinning. "It's not that bad."

"Your nose is red."

Daniel touched his nose self-consciously as he trotted up the last few steps side-by-side with Erik. He wasn't sure what the correct protocol was in this situation—a maybe first date with a quasi-foreign national. Should he greet him with a kiss on the cheek? They did the kiss on each cheek in France, Daniel remembered. But also in *The Godfather*, so maybe in Italy as well? Or was that only a Mafioso thing? In any case, Erik was definitely German, not French or Italian—nor, he hoped, a member of the Cosa Nostra.

On some of Daniel's other first dates, there'd been a quick and warm, yet chaste, kiss on the lips. Then there was the very memorable first date that had started with a blow job before the movie even began.

Daniel wasn't going to think about that one. Certainly not. And a blow job was certainly out of the question.

Erik solved the problem by leaning over and kissing Daniel lightly on the cheek. "And, also, hello."

"Hi," Daniel said, softly.

Erik pulled open one of the building's heavy front doors and led the way down the hall to a very noisy classroom. He smiled sheepishly. "Before we go in, I'll just say you can sit anywhere you like. And you can work with them, if you want. Or not. Whatever makes you comfortable.

"Welcome to Mrs. Thompson's third grade class. We're doing a series of workshops with them, and today, it's tool usage," Erik said over the excited hum of the eight-year-olds already hard at work with their brushes. He leaned in so Daniel could hear him better. "We buried a bunch of different things in blocks of plaster, and they have to excavate them. Next week, we'll study them together to theorize what the civilization that left them behind might be like."

"I think I found a diamond!" A young girl with braided hair shrieked and pointed at her block. "Erik! Come see!"

"Excuse me." Erik grinned. "I'm being paged."

"I'll just sit here and be decorative." Daniel waved at Antonio, who was working nearby and slipped into a seat next to a very serious-looking boy who was steadily brushing away at his block with his tongue firmly clenched between his teeth. Erik's right eye twitched in what might have been an amused wink. Chin in hand, Daniel watched him walk away and allowed himself a small dreamy sigh.

"You're blowing my dust around." The boy next to him frowned.

"Ooh, sorry. I'll try not to do that any more."

"And you don't have tools. Or a block."

"Oh, no, I'm just here to visit my friend." Daniel waved his hand nonchalantly.

"Antonio said everybody needs to have a block. And be doing work." The boy glared at him. "Not just goofing off."

"Oh, I'm sorry," Daniel said. "Where do you get the block and the tools?"

"Is this guy goofing off, Alan?" Erik reached over Daniel's shoulder and placed a block of plaster and a small bag of plastic chisels and paintbrushes in front of him. "Alan takes his work very seriously. He's going to be an archaeologist when he grows up."

"Really? That's cool!"

Alan looked up and beamed. "Yep. I'm gonna find dragon bones."

"Dinosaur bones?" Daniel asked.

"No." Alan goggled at him. "Dinosaurs are boring. I want to know why there are so many dragons in Norse mythology if there weren't actual dragons alive then for them to see and write about."

"Alan has some very interesting theories about dragons in ancient Scandinavia. He and I are going to research some of them," Erik explained.

"That's so cool." Daniel smiled as another child began yelling for Erik.

"You'd better get working on that block, Mr. Whitcomb." Erik put one hand on Daniel's shoulder. "I made that one especially for you." He walked away with another wink.

"Is it a diamond?" Daniel looked down at his block and opened the bag of tools. "I hope it's a diamond."

"It's not a diamond," Alan scoffed. "They probably don't have the budget to put diamonds in people's blocks."

Daniel chuckled at Alan's eight-year-old pragmatism. "You're probably right about that."

"Stacey Johnson thought she had a kazoo, which is just dumb." Alan brushed some plaster dust away with a small paintbrush. "Plaster gets poured into the mold, so it would have poured all over the kazoo and gotten inside it, and it would be ruined."

"Mmm," Daniel hummed, scraping a line into his block.

By five minutes before the end of the class, Daniel had heard Alan's opinions on the rest of Stacey Johnson's faults, proof of the existence of aliens and what they were having for lunch. He was also sneezing and covered in a very fine layer of white plaster dust. He did, however, have a good idea of the size and shape of the artifact buried in his block—a small, rectangular plastic cube stashed right in the center—but couldn't figure out what it signified.

"Should I be daring and just smash it out of the block?" he asked Alan.

"No." Alan shook his head. "Be careful. Go slowly."

"I can't stand it. I'm going to smash it."

"You're going to get in trouble."

With a surge of excitement he thought was ridiculous, Daniel grabbed his hammer and chipped away at the corners of the plaster surrounding his find. Once most of the plaster was gone, he used his fingers to break away the remaining chunks. His artifact was a small plastic box with a slightly domed lid.

"What do you suppose this is?" he asked Alan, who was absorbed in unearthing the last of the plastic bones in his block.

"It's a pirate treasure box, duh." Alan sniffed. "What's inside it?"

Daniel popped open the box top. Nestled inside was a Hershey's Kiss. He beamed at it. Erik had hidden a kiss in the block he'd made specifically for Daniel. *How incredibly adorable, and sweet and… dorky. Is this what swooning feels like?*

"What's inside?" Alan demanded.

Daniel clutched it to his chest. "A secret message. I have to go talk to Dr. Kappel after class."

"Cool." Alan dropped his tools in his box, swiped ineffectively at some of the plaster dust on the table and grabbed his pile of unearthed plastic bones. "See you, Daniel."

"Bye, Alan!"

Daniel lingered in his seat while the tumult of kids swirled around Erik and Antonio and out the door. As the last kids walked in a straggling line to their bus, Daniel walked slowly toward the front of the room where Erik and Antonio were beginning to clean up.

"Do you guys, um, need any help cleaning up?" Daniel shoved one hand in his jeans pocket and smiled hopefully.

"Thanks, Danny, but, as I was just telling Erik, I've got this." Antonio looked amused, then turned to glare at Erik. "Why don't you two get out of here?"

Erik flushed, but rubbed his hands together briskly. "I could show you where to wash your hands, maybe get some of this plaster dust off."

"Thanks," Daniel said, nodding. "That'd be nice."

He could swear Antonio winked at Erik as they walked out the door. He was surprised when Erik marched him past the door to the men's restroom, down the hallway and out the front door.

"I thought maybe you could wash your hands at the coffee shop in the student center?" Erik stammered as they went down the steps. "Maybe we could just have a cup of coffee or something? If you wanted to?"

"That'd be nice. I'd like that."

"Yeah?" Erik asked, his whole face relaxing into a wide relieved grin.

"Yeah. That'd be nice."

They walked slowly and silently down the sidewalk. It was nice. It was really nice. It was comfortable and warm, and Daniel felt bubbles rising up in his chest. Erik was something different.

"So," Daniel said. "You made that block of plaster for me?"

"Yeah." Erik nodded, smiling.

"You gave me a kiss."

"Too much? Too corny?"

"Definitely corny, and nerdy and amazing and wonderful. Definitely not too much. It was really sweet."

"You liked it?"

"Yeah. I like corny. I really like corny."

"Good to know." Erik stared down at his boots, still smiling.

"I mean, you know, you can kiss me," Daniel blurted. "Whenever you want to, or whatever."

Awesome, now he sounded like a blithering idiot. A *slutty* blithering idiot.

"That's also good to know," Erik replied. "I don't think I've quite worked up the courage again, but I'll let you know."

In the campus coffee shop they fell into easy conversation. They talked about their work, their friends, their families. Daniel found himself trying to tell stories in just the right way to make Erik laugh. They talked through "just a cup of coffee," through a lingering lunch, through a late afternoon snack, and straight into dinner at the diner down the street with Antonio and three of Erik's other colleagues.

With six people crammed into a booth meant for four, Daniel was pressed up against Erik for most of the meal; both of them chuckled at the awkwardness of trying to cut their food at the same time, reaching for the ketchup and nearly spilling each other's drinks. He was hyper-aware of Erik, of the hitch and steadying of Erik's breathing, the jostling of Erik's shoulders with his own, the pleasantly dark and woodsy scent of him as he moved. He liked the boisterous burst of Erik's laughter; he liked the quiet murmuring of Erik's voice in his ear explaining what someone was talking about; he liked the flashing interest of Erik's eyes as he talked about the morning class with the kids.

By the time dessert had been devoured and last cups of coffee had been drunk, Daniel was definitely head-over-heels smitten with Erik. His fingertips tingled, his toes tapped nervously and he had the unquenchable urge to throw Erik up against the nearest wall and kiss him silly, with groping hands and roaming tongues and the whole deal.

He caught Erik's eye and had to clear his throat abruptly. Daniel had to remember that, technically, they were on a first date. Maybe everything had gone sour with other guys because he'd been too eager, too easy. That seemed to make sense until Erik's thigh pressed against his, and Daniel began drumming his fingers on the table top just to relieve some of his jittering excitement.

As they all piled out of the booth, Erik paused to help Daniel put his coat on. He took Daniel's arm as they left the diner; they fell into step as they trailed behind the others.

"So, Antonio seems really nice," Daniel offered.

"Oh, Antonio's great. He's the first guy I met here, and he's just really... really helpful. Really funny, too."

"My best friend Kate is crazy about him."

"Yeah, I've heard a lot about her." Erik chuckled. "I think the feeling's mutual. He won't shut up about her sometimes."

They reached the stop just as a streetcar arrived; they got on and swiped their passes. They stood chatting about everything and nothing, laughing as they slid on the slushy floor as the streetcar lurched around corners.

Daniel sighed as they neared the Aberdeen Street station. "This is my stop. Where's yours?"

"Oh, uh." Erik laughed sheepishly. "Mine is about nine stops back that way."

"You live back near campus?"

"Yes. I meant to ask you if I could walk you home."

This guy just keeps getting more and more adorable and endearing, Daniel thought as they got off the train and walked toward Daniel's apartment a few blocks away.

"So, umm." Erik began as they stood on the sidewalk in front of Daniel's building. "I, I had a lot of fun tonight. Today. All day, with you, really."

Happiness fizzed under Daniel's skin. "Yeah, me too. We should definitely do it again."

"Yeah," Erik agreed, staring down at his boot scuffing at the cement. "We should."

"An official date, maybe? I'll pick you up, and we'll go out to dinner and a movie, or something?"

"What about tomorrow?" Erik blurted. "Are you busy tomorrow for dinner?"

"No." Daniel laughed. He probably should be more stand-offish, less available, less willing. But fuck the rules. "We could get lunch, even, if you wanted."

"Or breakfast." Erik grinned foolishly, then stopped blushing. "No, not—"

"Not breakfast." Daniel wanted Erik, god knew how badly, but this anticipation, this expectation and impatience to kiss him, touch him, feel him—this was almost incredible. "Not—yet."

"Not yet," Erik agreed, acknowledging the tension between them with a vague wave of his hand. "This is—intriguing. But not yet."

"I'm going to be completely old-fashioned and corny and say 'I want to get to know you better.'"

"That's not old-fashioned or corny. Or, even if it is, it's exactly what I was going to say."

"Okay, so—" Daniel grinned and leaned back against his front door. "I guess I'll see you tomorrow?"

"Yes." Erik sounded excited. "Tomorrow."

"I'll call you around ten, and we can plan lunch? Unless you'd rather do dinner?"

Erik laughed. "Lunch. Definitely lunch, first."

"Okay." Daniel's face was stuck in a huge grin. "Lunch. Tomorrow."

"Until tomorrow, Daniel." Erik smiled, then took a deep breath, spun on his heel and marched off.

TEN MONTHS BEFORE THE WEDDING

GOOD MORNING, DANIEL!

Congratulations on working out your budget! Good work! Your budget spreadsheet is saved! You've got a lot of decisions to make and we've got a lot to help you with, so let's get started! Thirty-seven new list items have been added to your master list. (*Research caterers, photographers, DJs and florists. Create specialized playlists for reception DJs. Reserve your date and venue. Click here for more.*)

What's trending on Aurora? Hot Right Now: Invite the Celestial Heavens to Your Wedding With Glow-in-the-Dark Bridesmaid Dresses! Click here to read the article about your next wedding must-have!

Have a great day, Daniel!

Love,
Aurora

**

Click on checkboxes to mark task as complete, or on task name to edit/modify.
Unsubscribe from reminders.

TWO DAYS OF BANTERING ABOUT wedding possibilities and the only thing they'd been able to check off the list was their budget. Thinking about the credit card debt they would soon be swimming in made Daniel feel nauseated.

"Let's remember that this number represents the maximum value of this range," Erik said. "We should aim to stay as close to the minimum value as possible."

"I mean, we don't even really know how much all this costs." Daniel picked at the fringe on the throw pillow under his head. "Maybe we'll be really pleasantly surprised. Maybe it's not going to be that bad."

"When I helped plan the anthropology department annual dinner last year, it was close to ten thousand dollars. And that's dinner, the tables, the plates and silverware and people to serve it all."

"Hmm."

"Yeah, let's not go that high, hmm?" Erik said.

"I'm thinking big-budget weddings are pretentious, anyway, right? And impersonal. Who really feels like releasing live doves is a good way to commemorate your special day? Who the hell honestly likes doves?" Daniel threw the wedding magazine down on the floor at Erik's feet.

"Dove breeders, probably," Erik said as he flipped through the pages of his notes for tomorrow's lecture.

"Smartass." Daniel sat up and shoveled salsa onto a chip from the bowls on the coffee table. Neither of them wanted to cook after a long day: Erik wrangling freshmen through their first field trip to a dig site, and Daniel dealing with the chaos caused by an overly-carbonated batch of Stefan's homemade kombucha exploding over a several boxes of Stasia's handspun yarn. They were really going to have to do something about storage in the back room of Co-Op.

"Okay, so we have a budget," Daniel said around a mouthful of chip. "Now we need a date. Like, real wedding date, so we can start actually planning things and signing contracts and—"

"Yes, but we don't really know what venues will be available, what church or what restaurant or whatever you've dreamed of—"

"What church? I mean, there must be hundreds of churches in the city? How do we choose?"

"We could start with brainstorming ideas for which areas of the city we like."

Daniel grabbed a notepad and began scribbling ideas. "Shreveston—"

"Everything will cost quadruple the price in Shreveston."

"Yes, but they've got the best of everything."

"What about Buryport?" Erik offered as he rummaged in the bag of chips.

"Oh, my god, are you serious? You want our guests to get mugged?" Daniel shook his head and continued to scribble.

"Oh, don't be a snob. It's not that bad. And we could have it at St. Cecilia's."

"No. Just, no. There's not a good reception site anywhere nearby, not even a decent restaurant. Trust me, I know." Daniel tapped his pen on the pad. "I mean, if we could find something in Tallen Village, that would be ideal. But I don't know if there's anything there that would work." Daniel hummed as he chewed the top of his pen.

"What about Panama Alley?"

"Well, that would be fabulous. Except I don't think my mother is going to be thrilled with her son getting married at The Log Jam."

"There are plenty of places in Panama Alley that are not so—"

"Gay," Daniel finished. "I know. It's a great place to be, but if my mother has to walk past a bar called Manhole to get to the reception, she's going to have a stroke."

"Your mother wouldn't even take the time to realize that Manhole is a gay bar."

Daniel smirked. "That's true. She'd wonder why we're having our reception near a construction supply store."

"What if we come up with where we'd like our reception, and then pick someplace to have the ceremony near there?" Erik sat up, setting his class notes to the side.

"Oh god, yes. It would be awful to have to drive an hour to get to the reception."

"Okay, then where are we going to have the reception?"

"Dance club? Event space? Restaurant?" Daniel said.

"But what restaurant?"

"There's that Lebanese place on Seventh. They have that big banquet room that would be perfect." Daniel doodled in the margin of the page.

"Or there's the Royal Hotel," Erik suggested, taking a swig of beer.

"Oh, the Royal. That would be amazing, wouldn't it?" Daniel sighed as he leaned back, propping his head on the back of the couch.

"Could we do the ceremony there, too? In the same space?"

"I—I have no idea. I guess I'd have to ask? I mean, probably, right?"

"Okay, so we go with whatever date the Royal has available," Erik said.

"And *if* it's in our budget. I mean, it might be ridiculously expensive."

"It's going to be ridiculously expensive, Daniel. It's the Royal Hotel."

"Well, maybe we should have a backup plan," Daniel said.

"Yes, obviously."

"Okay, so, we go with the Royal Hotel, *if* it's in our budget and *if* they have a date available before August—"

"Before July, babe," Erik said, finishing his beer. "If I get any of these grants I'm applying for, I'll be on a dig by July."

"Okay, so, we go with the Royal Hotel, *if* it's in our budget and *if* they have a date available before July—so long as it's not a weird date, like a Wednesday morning. That's just not going to work."

"Right. Not Wednesday morning."

"So what's the backup plan?" Daniel asked.

"I guess we start looking at places where we could have the ceremony that might be available? And that aren't too far away from the reception site."

"Okay, so—oh god. Do we choose a date, and look for places to have it? Or do we look for places to have it, and then choose a date?"

"Yes." Erik said wryly.

"That is not helpful." Daniel playfully shoved a chip in Erik's mouth; he grimaced and began chewing.

"How the fuck are we supposed to make this decision?"

Erik shrugged his shoulders and rolled his eyes, before swallowing with exaggerated effort.

"I don't have a fucking clue. But is there any more beer in the fridge?"

"I don't know," Daniel said as he scrolled through lists on the wedding app on his phone.

"No beer in the fridge," Erik called from the kitchen. "But there's some in the cupboard."

"So drink it."

"Drink warm beer? What, do you think I'm from England or something? I would never."

"Snob."

Erik sat back down next to him and offered him a can of Coke. "I have standards."

"Ooh, could we have it at the museum?"

"Probably. They do special events, dinners and banquets and stuff."

"And you'd probably get a discount, being a faculty member, right?" Daniel asked.

"I could check. But, yes, it's a possibility."

"How romantic! Getting married in the Egyptian section, right next to all the mummies."

"You are so strange sometimes," Erik said.

"And you love me."

"Yes, I do."

THREE YEARS AGO

Erik realized he was in love with Daniel only a few weeks after they met. He was surprised by the revelation and more than a little unnerved.

He'd asked to see some of Danny's glasswork, and, after showing off some of his lamps and jewelry, Daniel had asked if he'd like to see some more.

Erik was surprised when Daniel led him out the door and down the street, past the little shops and restaurants he was familiar with, to a small and sunny park in front of St. Cecilia's.

"A church?" Erik asked.

"I—I used to come here—a lot, when I was younger." Daniel gestured vaguely. "And then, when I got older, one of their windows got smashed, so they let me make the replacement."

Erik shoved his hands in his jeans pockets and smiled. Danny looked soft and rumpled and cuddly in his battered jeans and old T-shirt. Erik was torn between wanting to take him home and make him lunch and wanting to take him home and kiss him until they both wound up naked.

"Would you like to see it?" Daniel asked.

"Of course."

Daniel smiled and reached for Erik's hand. His smile widened when Erik laced his fingers through Daniel's and swung their hands between them.

Daniel towed him to one of the side doors, and they slipped inside the dark, quiet church. They walked down a hallway and past a desk, where an elderly woman sat with her glasses perched on the end of her nose as she typed.

"Hi, Gloria," Daniel said, giggling as the woman jumped slightly in surprise. "Sorry, I didn't mean to startle you."

"Oh, Daniel!" she said. "Hello, sweetheart! It's been ages since we've seen you."

"I know." Daniel smiled. "I've been busy."

"Well, you march yourself right over here and give me a hug. I have missed you, young man."

Daniel blushed, but bent to give the frail woman a hug. He towered over her. Erik noticed Daniel closed his eyes with a quiet smile as she held him an extra moment.

"Oh, now, that's my boy," she said, patting his arm as he stood up.

"I'm actually here to show off, Gloria. This is my—my friend, Erik, and I'd like to show him the window, if that's okay."

"Hello, Erik." Gloria looked delighted to see him. "I'm Gloria Bidwell, the church secretary. I've been keeping my eye on this scalawag here since he was born. Now, have you ever seen our Daniel's window? It's glorious. It's magnificent. We're all so proud of him. And not just for making such a beautiful window. He's grown into such a fine young man."

"Thanks, Gloria." Daniel smiled again.

"Father Tim will be so sad he missed you today. He's off visiting parishioners at the hospitals."

"I'll stop by again soon."

"He'll be delighted to see you," she said.

Gloria made her way around the desk. "I've got to visit the powder room myself, so you boys will just have to find your own way. Choir practice starts in forty-five minutes."

"Then we will get out of here pronto." Daniel grinned.

"Oh, you," she admonished, affectionately. "They're all just happy to see you."

"Mother hens, all of them. I'll never get out with my dignity intact."

"Maybe we should stay longer," Erik teased. "That might be something to see."

"Oh, they'd be delighted to meet you, Erik." Gloria took his arm as they walked slowly down the rest of the hallway. "They're all anxious to see our Daniel happy."

"Well, not *all* of them," Daniel muttered.

"No, not all of them," she agreed. "But God will judge them for their arrogance and their hatred and their inability to love, Danny. Don't you worry. They'll get their come-uppance."

"That doesn't sound like a good church-going lady."

Gloria laughed. "Why do you think I work at the church? I need all the help I can get!"

She was still laughing when they reached the ladies room. "Now, you boys go have fun." As she held onto the door handle, she held her wrinkled cheek up to them. "Give this old lady a kiss goodbye, both of you."

Erik kissed her cheek. "It was nice to meet you."

"And it was nice to meet you, too, Erik. I hope you'll come back again soon."

As he watched Gloria beam up at Erik, Daniel noticed Erik's gentle look.

Daniel grinned and kissed her cheek loudly with a smack. "Love you, Gloria."

"I love you, too, my Danny Boy. God bless you." She patted him on the arm and lowered her voice to a stage whisper. "And, you keep track of this one, Danny. He's a good man. And ooh boy, he's a looker."

Erik pretended not to hear her, as Daniel sputtered with laughter. "Okay, Gloria. I'll see what I can do."

Still laughing, Daniel slowly walked him past the large center aisle with its view of the sanctuary and steered him down the smaller side aisle.

"She seems like a lovely woman," Erik said.

"Oh, Gloria's the best. Heart of gold, tongue of steel. She loves people with all her heart, but man, if you step out of line, she will not hesitate to let you know about it."

"She thinks you're wonderful."

"Yeah, well." Daniel sighed. "She's always been a good friend of mine, ever since I was little kid. She and Father Brian were why I've kept coming back here."

"Father Brian?"

"Yeah. He kind of, kept track of me when I was kid. He was my friend and he always was interested in what I was doing, and how things were going. If I was having trouble with my family, or with school, or just anything, I could always come to Father Brian and talk my way through it, and he'd help me figure out what to do. He died actually right before I finished the window, of cancer."

"He didn't get to see the window?"

"Not completed, no." Daniel tapped on the side of the pew as they walked. "I mean, he saw the sketches and the designs, and some of the work. But no. He never saw the whole window."

They continued down the aisle, past the uncomfortable-looking wooden benches and their racks of Bibles and hymnals.

"This side of the church overlooks the rectory's yard—that's where Father Tim lives," Daniel whispered. "In fact, it looks almost directly into the rectory's downstairs bathroom."

He made a playfully horrified face. "So, while it would have been nice to have some lighter, more translucent colors to let some more natural light in here, the powers-that-be opted *not* to see Father Tim's ass during choir rehearsal."

They stopped close to the far corner of the church in a dark chapel. The stained glass window was one of most beautiful things Erik had seen, even compared to the windows in all the churches in France and Italy his mother had dragged him to.

A single figure stood at the center—a woman draped in deep blue robes, which were here and there speckled with gold. All around her was a riot of color: reds and golds and oranges at the top slowly blending down into yellows and greens, which melted down into purples and blues that faded into the hem of her robe. The pieces of glass making up the window were so small, and the color variations so subtle it took a moment for Erik to realize what he was looking at.

"A rainbow?"

"Yeah." Daniel sat down on the bench closest to the window, looking up at it. "I had been thinking about that Noah's Ark story and the rainbow after the flood being kind of promise. You know, like, no matter what, no matter how angry anyone gets or how bad things are, there's always going to be someone there who cares. There's always someone who's on your team, on your side. Somewhere out there, there's always someone who loves you, even if you don't know it."

Erik only vaguely remembered the biblical story, but was fairly certain there was more to it than that. He was more interested in this glimpse into Daniel's thought process, what Daniel took away from the story. Since meeting Daniel, Erik had spent a great deal of his time baffled; Daniel never quite did what Erik expected.

"And not a rainbow as a subversive gay motif?"

"Nah." Daniel chuckled. "I mean, not consciously or anything." He sniffed and shook his head, still looking up at the window. "It took me weeks to get her face the way I wanted."

Erik stepped closer to look up at the Madonna. Instead of the demure, downcast eyes and the resigned, half-bored simper he was used to seeing, her face was alive, vibrant and delighted.

He'd seen that smile on his mother's face when she'd picked him up at the airport, and on his sister's face when she marched to the stage for her diploma from medical school. It was the gentle smile just before one can't keep joy inside any longer, the split-second before lips change from a delighted smile to a teeth-baring full-force grin of happiness.

The Madonna's eyes were different, too. She appeared to be looking directly at him, delighted with what she saw.

"She's watching me," Erik mock-whispered.

Daniel's laugh echoed across the church.

Erik stepped to the side. "Her eyes are following me."

"That," Daniel explained, "is just an added bonus. I didn't mean for that to happen."

"She looks like a nice lady. Someone I'd want to know."

"Thanks." Daniels grinned.

"She wants me to know everything is going to be okay," Erik said.

Daniel turned to stare at him, an amazed look on his face. "That's exactly what I was going for."

"Well, you got it. It's really—it's amazing, Daniel."

Daniel smiled that little smile, the one that made him look as if he was glowing.

"This is my favorite time of day to come see her," Daniel said. "In the afternoon, like this, the light coming in is indirect and all diffused and really mellow. It makes her really—chill and relaxed and welcoming."

"She's not like this all the time?"

"No." Daniel chuckled. "In the morning, when she's got direct light streaming through, she's kind of all—'Yeah! Go! You can do it! You're awesome! Get out there and show them what you can do!'"

Erik laughed. "How long did it take you?"

"Total? Over a year."

Erik looked up at the window again and shook his head in amazement.

"I didn't really have anything else to do. I—I didn't get into the schools I applied to and it really threw me for a loop. Everyone else went away to college, and I was just stuck here, you know?"

"You made this, by yourself, when you were eighteen?"

"Yeah." Daniel rubbed the back of his neck. "More like nineteen, I guess."

"Holy shit, Daniel. That's amazing!"

"Well, I didn't really have anything else. Father Brian got me the job. I used to come here to youth group and stuff, but mostly I got the job because I could do it for basically the cost of the materials."

"You did this for free?"

"This place meant a lot to me, growing up. Having a place I could go if I needed something, if I needed help. There was always someone here for me when I was having trouble. And it meant a lot to me. I wanted to help make it a place like that for someone else, if they needed it. That's what was driving me, you know? Maybe helping someone else with what I could do. Maybe someone else would see her and be a little bit more hopeful, or comforted, or something. Someone will see her and know there's always someone out there for them."

Erik stepped back and stared at the window again. Daniel had created this, all on his own, when he was nineteen years old. He'd lost his mentor, perhaps someone he'd felt was a replacement father figure, certainly one of the few people who seemed to support him wholeheartedly and without reservation. He'd lost him before it was finished, and the thought of that made Erik's heart hurt. Daniel had made this window, this gorgeous piece of work, to remind others, and himself, that somewhere there was someone else out there who loved you.

OUTSIDE, THEY BLINKED IN THE bright sunlight and laughed at the funny faces the other was making. It was a slow Saturday afternoon. Kids played in the park nearby, people ran errands, but no one moved quickly.

Daniel glowed. Peace and contentment and ease flowed from him, and Erik grinned as he took Daniel's hand in an effort to feel some of that relaxation.

Erik was in love with Daniel. It'd only been a few weeks, but Daniel enveloped Erik in a cheerful, happy world that Erik didn't normally see. He found he liked feeling playful, that he liked the jokes that popped into his head to make Daniel laugh, that he liked to feel his own laughter bubbling nearly at the surface of his skin.

He was in love, and it'd only been a few weeks, yet he couldn't quite let go enough to admit it, at least not out loud, and certainly not to Daniel. In a few more weeks, maybe a few more months, he'd be ready to tell Daniel.

NINE MONTHS BEFORE THE WEDDING

GOOD MORNING, DANIEL!

Congratulations on booking your officiant and venue! Good work! Your contact details are saved! Seventeen more items have been added to your checklist. (Compile guest food allergy database. Book your caterer and begin planning menu., Coordinate bridal party colors. Click here for more.)

☑ Click here to add or modify list entries. Showing 1-6 out of 70 checklist entries left to complete.

What's trending on Aurora? Hot Right Now: Tennis Playing Chippendales Themed Weddings – The Balls are in Your Court! Click here to read the article about your next wedding must-have!

Have a great day, Daniel!

Love,
Aurora

"I THINK AURORA IS DISAPPOINTED in me."

"What?" Erik rubbed at his eye. It wasn't even early morning, judging by the weak light coming through the blinds from the streetlights. "Who?"

"Aurora. The wedding planning app." Daniel lay on his back, wide awake and staring up at the ceiling.

"The wedding planning app is not a sentient being. It has no feelings or opinions."

"I feel like she's judging me. I'm sorry if I woke you up."

"Oh my god, go to sleep."

"I can't. I'm never going to sleep ever again." Daniel tugged the blanket higher up his chest, folding his arms over it and exhaling heavily.

"You're being dramatic."

"I've got too many things buzzing in my head. There's too many things I'm going to forget to do."

"I thought that's why you had that damn app, so you don't have to remember anything; it's all right there saved on your tablet."

"Yes, but I have to *remember* to put everything in it." Daniel rolled over. "She doesn't just know everything—"

"A: She is not a she. *It* is an *it*. B: What are we doing tomorrow?"

"Oh my god, what is the point of sharing the app calendar if you're never going to look at it?" Daniel wailed.

"I look at it. It's just crammed so full of everything that I have no idea what's going on when."

Daniel blew out his breath. "Look, I know you don't like the calendar. We've been over that, but I don't know how else to keep track of all of these appointments and deadlines."

"I told you, we could color-code them, or something," Erik rolled to his side and punched at his pillow.

"Aurora doesn't give you that option."

"Well, it should."

"I agree, but there's nothing I can do about that." Daniel bunched his pillow up under his head. "Tomorrow, we have four appointments to meet with caterers: two in the morning, two in the afternoon."

"Why so many in one day?"

"It's the only day we both have available this week, and I am not going to make any decisions about the food at our reception without you there to discuss it."

"Seriously, you could just make a choice, and I'll live with it." Erik rolled over.

"I don't want you to just 'live with it,' Erik." Daniel tried to keep his voice neutral, but failed. "This is our wedding. I don't want you to just 'live with it.'"

"Why are you getting so worked up about it?"

"We only get one chance at this. Everything needs to be perfect."

"You're going to drive us both crazy, you know that, right?" Erik tugged the blankets back up over his shoulder.

"Well, then, we'll both be crazy." Daniel squinted up at the ceiling. He was so tired of making these decisions. Why were there so many options? Why were there so many decisions? The planning was getting on Erik's nerves; *he* was getting on Erik's nerves. Erik was getting on his nerves. They were both just a pile of irritated nerves because the to-do list didn't seem to be getting any smaller.

Daniel's phone chimed with another notification from Aurora.

New Private Message from: MommyMargie.

His mother probably had another ludicrous suggestion for the reception, or a passive-aggressive reminder of the hymn that she and his father had had played at *their* wedding, that their grandparents had had played at *their* wedding and that she expected to hear at *his* wedding. Or maybe his parents had decided to paint the living room green. Who knew?

Daniel rubbed his eyes and swung his legs out of bed. He wouldn't get any more sleep; he couldn't avoid dealing with his family, because that only made them more rabid. He pulled on his sweatshirt and shuffled out to the living room to start his day, pretending he didn't hear Erik's frustrated sigh.

THEY WEREN'T IMPRESSED WITH ANY of the caterers they met that day.

"Baked chicken breast? Chickpea tagine?" Daniel asked as they got back his apartment. "I mean, really? None of them sounded appetizing to me."

"The tagine might work. Or maybe a nice curry? Maybe we could do an international menu?"

"We should just give up and do sausages and sauerkraut."

"I wouldn't argue with you. Your mother will pitch a fit, but I won't." Erik chuckled.

"Maybe we *could* do German food? A nod to your heritage, or something like that."

"Maybe," Erik said.

"Let's do some research on that." Daniel dropped his bag next to his worktable. "I've got to sketch these windows, and then maybe we can work on that later."

One of Daniel's professors had recommended him to Mrs. Reinholt, an older woman renovating one of the historic homes in Shreveston, an upscale area of Tallenburg. She wanted it filled with windows in the style of Frank Lloyd Wright: geometric shapes and unexpected colors.

Daniel grabbed one of his reference books. He flipped through the sections on Wright and on Kandinsky, one of his favorite artists, for inspiration. He pulled out his colored pencils, compass and ruler. He would work through the actual design on his computer; it was easier to resize shapes and come up with exact color combinations. But when he was just beginning, he liked to sketch by hand.

Daniel carefully traced circles, bisecting lines, intersections and angles. Sketching was a form of meditation for him. He hummed as he began to let his mind wander and relax. But today, his drawing practice could not entirely block out the noise in his mind. Worries about the wedding kept popping into his head, demanding that he figure out one problem or another immediately. *What are we going to do about a DJ? Who is going to be in our wedding party? What about the seating arrangements? I can't forget that I absolutely can't have my mother's friend, Mrs. Cunningham, anywhere near Uncle Timothy's new wife or there will be fireworks.*

He put on his headphones and set his iPod to shuffle songs. He sunk deeper and deeper into his sketching. Erik interrupted only once, touching his shoulder gently and pointing toward the kitchen where he'd made Daniel a sandwich for dinner. Daniel smiled up at him and gestured toward the sketches spread all over the table.

"I know." Erik kissed his forehead. "Keep going, there's some really great stuff in there. I'm going to meet Antonio to talk over some work things, but I'll be back around ten, okay?"

"'Kay," Daniel murmured as he stretched his neck and shoulders. "Love you."

"Love you, too. Don't forget to eat, okay?"

"I'll try not to." Daniel's smile was more relaxed than it had been in weeks. The tightness in his shoulders and his stress headache were gone, replaced by welcome tension in his arms and neck; his muscles were not accustomed to being bent over a design for so long. He hadn't sketched like this in ages. He'd have to start doing some yoga before he started actually making these windows, or he might wind up a pretzel.

THREE YEARS AGO

Like most people, Daniel had his strange assortment of random acquisitions, but Erik was a collector—an avid collector.

Erik lived in a tiny two-room apartment on the first floor of one of the older university dormitories, which the university provided as part of his compensation.

"Yeah, it's supposed to be for the dorm mother, or something like that," Erik explained as he led Daniel down the long hallway to his apartment. They'd gone out several times in the three weeks since they'd met, and Daniel had never been to Erik's place.

"I believe they're called RAs, or Resident Assistants, now." Daniel smiled, and Erik flushed as he unlocked his front door. They'd been out to dinner, and the subject of hobbies had come up. Erik wanted to show Daniel his collection. Had it been any other man, Daniel would have sworn that was a euphemism for "dick." But this was Erik, and so Daniel wasn't at all sure what was behind his suggestion.

"Well, I don't have to do any of that stuff. No 'Rah-rah, yay, you're in college now' kinds of things. Or busting underage kids for having alcohol in their rooms, or anything like that." Erik opened his door with a flourish and ushered Daniel in. "It's not much, but it's home, for now."

The front door opened into an area that served as living room, dining room and kitchen. A low coffee table sat in front of a leather couch from the 50s, with a leather club chair at the end. A rickety-looking table and one chair sat in the opposite corner, next to a very small electric stove with a countertop, miniature refrigerator and sink beside it.

Erik led him toward the bedroom. "Okay, I swear, I'm not trying to make a move on you—"

"And why the hell not?" Daniel said, flirtatiously.

Erik flushed again, cleared his throat loudly and flicked on the bedroom light. The bed under the window had been carefully and precisely made. Aside from a small chest of drawers, the rest of the room was full of bookcases neatly arranged like library shelves. Piles of magazines lay flat, each carefully wrapped in special archival paper. Small cardboard tabs protruded from some of the stacks.

Daniel touched the stacks lightly. "These are comic books?"

"Pulp magazines," Erik said, proudly. "*Amazing Tales, Phenomenal Stories*—they're all short story collections from the 1930s and 40s— some from the 50s, as well. These are all mostly science fiction."

"Science fiction short stories? Like, Isaac Asimov?" Daniel vaguely remembered the name from a college class.

"Asimov, yes. I don't collect *him*, in particular. I collect another author. But, yes, stories like his."

"Science fiction from the 40s and 50s? Like, robots and stuff?" Daniel was amused. Erik's bashful pride in his collection made Daniel want to throw him down on the couch and kiss him.

"People collect these for various reasons, but I collect the stories of Timothy McMurphy, who wrote under several pseudonyms for several publications. Jack Bronner, Victor Krueger and Dorothy Tomlinson, among others." In the short time they'd been dating, Daniel had begun to recognize Erik's "Professor Mode:" earnest, serious and irresistible.

He couldn't take it anymore; the strain of *not* kissing Erik was rasping at him. Every time they'd been out, it had been a confusing swirl of maybe-it's-date, maybe-it's-not. Erik had talked it over and over with Kate—what she thought (yes, they're dating and ridiculous for not having kissed yet), what she could pull of out Antonio (not much, Antonio being reluctant to dish about his friend's purported love life), what her gossipy friends from work thought (date him, screw him, give us salacious details). He just couldn't take the suspense and uncertainty anymore. If these weren't dates, and kissing Erik was a huge mistake— well then, at least he'd know for sure. And if they *were* dates, ohh the fun they could begin to have.

He leaned forward and pressed their lips together in a slightly awkward first kiss. After a stunned moment, Erik kissed him back, somewhat chastely at first, then more and more hungrily. His hands came up to grip the muscles at the small of Daniel's back.

When he was mere seconds away from tearing off all Erik's clothing and having him right there on the floor, Daniel pulled away, breathing hard. His previous first kisses had never been this intense.

"You collect stories by a male author named Dorothy?" Daniel raised his eyebrows and turned to toy with a button on Erik's shirt. He needed some time to catch his breath.

"Yes, Dorothy." Erik chuckled. "He's not as famous as Asimov, of course, but he's becoming more and more popular. Sometimes there's quite a bidding war to get some of these."

Daniel hummed. "And what does your Dorothy write about?"

"He usually writes detective stories that are solved with a science, but, fantastical science, you know?"

"No?" Daniel smiled.

"The answer to the mystery always involves something like a chemical compound called—hmm. Like, 'phosphorescent dynatricin.'"

"Which isn't a real chemical—"

"No. But it vaguely sounds enough like one that readers will accept it as one."

Daniel glanced at the bed with his eyebrow raised and bit his lip. Erik grinned and took Daniel's hand, tugging him out of the bedroom and over toward the vintage leather couch.

"My favorite story of his involves a stolen crate of methylitic carbonate—"

Daniel pushed him down on the couch, faced him and bracketed Erik's knees with his own. If Erik wanted to hold off on vaulting into bed with each other, Daniel was absolutely fine with that. So long as he got to put his lips back together with Erik's—he was fine. Long and slow, passionate make-outs on the couch could be nice, too. Very nice, indeed.

"You are a nerd," Daniel murmured as he bent to kiss him. "An adorable nerd and I like hearing you talk like this."

Erik chuckled, low and rough. "Then let me tell you about the one with the doomsday machine called the Tryptometric Filotron."

"Oh god, yes."

FOUR MONTHS LATER, THE ACCUMULATION from two collector's shows at the civic center and a late-night online buying spree threatened to overwhelm Erik's tiny apartment. Boxes of vintage magazines were stacked in every available space: in corners, on chairs, at the small tables. Erik's magazines were, in Daniel's mind, going to be one of the major hurdles to overcome, should he and Erik ever decide to move in together. They spent most nights together, either here or at Daniel's apartment, but the magazine collection seemed to need a lot more attention than Daniel thought it warranted.

"Erik," he called from the front door. "Another package for you."

He turned, glowered at the box the mailman had handed him and searched for a place to put it. They were supposed to be going out to dinner, but Erik's office hours at the university had run long, and they were late.

Erik poked his head out of the tiny bedroom where he'd been getting dressed. "Thanks, babe. Just put it anywhere."

"There's no more 'anywhere' free," Daniel grumbled as he tried to balance the box on a stack of similar boxes near the door. The stack toppled with a thud and Daniel yelped as he tried to jump out of its path.

"What's going on out there?" Erik emerged from the bedroom, finally dressed and untangling his suspenders as he pulled them up over his shoulders.

"Your apartment is trying to kill me," Daniel said as he tried unsuccessfully to restack the boxes.

"Careful!" Erik said.

"I'm trying to be careful, Erik." Daniel was annoyed. Erik had been cranky for days and Daniel's patience was at an all-time low.

"You just can't throw these around." Erik pushed past him and carefully placed one box on top of another.

"You have got to get rid of these boxes. This is ridiculous."

"I can't shelve them until they've been catalogued—"

"Well, catalog them."

"It's been driving me crazy, you know, but my time for doing things like cataloguing has been taken up recently," Erik smiled tightly.

"I'm sorry; I am taking up too much of your time?"

"That isn't what I said—"

"That's *exactly* what you said."

"You know what I mean, Daniel."

"No, I don't."

"Stop being argumentative." Erik moved quickly toward the kitchen.

"I am not being argumentative." Daniel's pulse sped up. "You just implied that I'm taking up so much of your time that it's driving you crazy."

"I am happy having you taking up my time. But you *are* driving me crazy right now."

"Nice." *This evening has been a disaster from the start.*

"Just—" Erik paused and went to sit at his tiny kitchen table. "Let's stop this and have a rational discussion."

"Oh, so now I'm irrational?"

Erik took a deep breath and blew it out explosively. He put his hands flat on the table in front of him and flexed his fingers into it. "I didn't say that," he growled.

"You implied it."

"You're so caught up in what you think I'm *implying*. How about *listening* to what I am actually saying, for once—"

"For once?" Daniel wanted to laugh. This is exactly how he expected tonight to go. In fact, he'd been expecting this fight, or a fight like it, for weeks.

"Look, I don't even—I don't know what to do here. I don't know how to—I just think it would be better if we—"

"If you say 'spend some time apart,'" Daniel snarled.

"I don't mean—I don't want—"

"Just spit it out, Erik. If we're going to do this, let's just get it over with."

"Stop escalating this, just stop it." Erik raised his voice. "That's not— I'm not—Christ, you're infuriating."

"Just add that to my list of sins." If they were going to break up, Daniel wanted it over with.

"I can't talk with you like this!" Erik yelled so loudly Daniel thought he could hear it echo across the apartment.

"So, you're going to yell, instead?"

"I'm *not* going to talk with you like this." Erik stood up scraping his chair back so roughly it tottered. He walked purposefully toward the door and grabbed his jacket from the hook in the hallway.

"Where are you going?"

"I don't know. Out." Erik slammed the door behind him.

Well, this was something new. Daniel had been through breakups before—some more memorable than others. Some had been a relief, or he'd barely noticed—Roderigo, Steve, Mac—and others had been scarring—but he wasn't going to think about Matthew right now.

Breakups weren't new, but what *was* new was breaking up in someone else's apartment and then being left alone in said person's apartment. He wasn't quite sure what to do next, what the protocol should be. He just didn't know what to do.

Numbness settled over him—a bleak view of the events to come, unfolding in crystal clear, black and white sharpness.

When he left Erik's apartment, he would not be coming back. Did he have his keys to his apartment still in his pocket? His wallet and phone? It would be just his luck to be dumped, leave as gracefully as he could—head held high—and have to crawl back and sit waiting on the steps outside for whenever Erik decided to come back, just so he could ask for his keys.

He slapped at his pockets—wallet, keys, phone, all accounted for. Was there anything else here that he would regret leaving behind and never seeing again?

No, he was fairly certain there was nothing here of his, and, if he couldn't remember it, then it probably wasn't that important. Nothing here he couldn't leave behind. At least, nothing he would miss.

Except Erik.

He slapped that thought down like a mosquito about to bite him. *Not now, Whitcomb. Not here.*

He checked his pockets one last time: his wallet, phone and keys hadn't moved in the past fifteen seconds. He pushed his chair into the table and turned out the lights. Ex-boyfriend or not, Daniel didn't want to add to Erik's electric bill.

He stood in the darkened hallway, taking in the familiar aromas one last time: the leather smell of Erik's armchair by the window, the slightly vinegary scent of old paper and the faint citrus smell from the bowl of oranges on the counter.

"Goodbye," he whispered, perhaps somewhat theatrically. Theatricality made a moment real, and he'd be glad later that he'd taken the time to acknowledge this end. He carefully pulled the front door closed behind him.

Daniel walked down the stairs slowly, planning his next move. He was always proud of how he handled breakups, at least in Stage One. Kate had called Stage One his "Ice Queen Mode" since they were kids. He would be calm, cool, collected and unemotional. Vicious at times, if provoked, but generally placid.

In preparation for Stage Two, he would stop at the grocery store, stock up on frozen pizza, macaroni and cheese ingredients and other foods he could make with minimal effort. And alcohol. And ice cream. Stage Two definitely called for alcohol and ice cream.

In Stage Two, Kate referred to Daniel as a "blubbering pile of pathetic broken-heartedness." She had always had such a way with words. He wouldn't call her until Stage Two had well and truly begun. It usually began when he was packing whatever belongings of The Ex were left at his apartment, or packing up mementos and photos from their time together. *I'd better get a start on that as soon as I get back to my apartment.*

Daniel struggled with too many bags as he left the grocery store, shuffled down the sidewalk and struggled with the bags again as he walked up the stairs to his apartment. He dropped a bag as he unlocked the door and swore softly as he pushed it through his front door with his foot.

He put everything away tidily, pleased at how responsible and unaffected he seemed. When the pasta he'd started cooking was almost ready, he walked into his living room, taking mental note of things he'd have to decide what to do with. Everywhere he looked, there was something of Erik's: a sweater draped on the back of the couch, a notebook full of his lecture notes on the coffee table, a pair of thick wool socks curled up under the corner of the bed and just visible through the bedroom doorway. He glanced at the wall behind his desk where several photos of the two of them were pinned up, then at a postcard on the fridge door from the weekend they'd spent in Boston.

Daniel took a deep breath. Dinner would be ready soon, and he'd start packing up Erik's things after he ate. He poured himself a glass of wine, leaving the vodka and rum for Stage Two, and finished making his dinner.

He sat down at his little table with a real napkin and a fork, even some peas as a side dish, and with his refilled glass of wine sitting next to his glass of water. He sighed, impressed with himself at how together he was. Surely this was progress? Surely this was maturity? This breakup was so different from the last one he'd been through. He'd been a wreck, an inconsolable heap of misery. Stage Two had started early that time, with a vengeance.

A sudden banging on his front door startled him and sent the peas flying off his fork. He rushed to open the door. His mouth dropped open with confusion and a frisson of delight when he saw Erik standing there, out of breath, cradling a large plastic bag of what appeared to be takeout boxes.

"What the fuck are you doing here?" Erik demanded.

"This is my apartment. Where else would I be?"

"No, I mean, why the fuck aren't you at my place?"

"I—you—you're the one who broke up with *me,* dude. I should be asking you why the fuck *you're* at *my* apartment—"

"I—broke up with you?" The plastic bag rustled as Erik tried to catch his breath.

"Yeah, you stormed out of your apartment after saying you weren't going to talk to me—"

"I wasn't breaking up with you, you jackass. I just—you got me so mad, I needed to clear my head."

"You weren't breaking—"

"No!" Erik shouted. "Christ, why would I break up with you?"

"Because you're sick of me? You're tired of not having any time to yourself? You're tired of having me around?"

"Fuck no, Danny. Just, fuck no. I am never tired of you."

"But then—" Daniel was caught entirely off-guard, absolutely unsure of what was happening.

"Look, I knew my class running over was a bad thing. You eat lunch so early on Thursdays, and I knew you'd be hungry and you get so cranky when you're hungry—"

"I do not—"

"Do we have to do this in the hallway?" Erik shrugged his shoulders, offering up the plastic bag in his arms. "I've got dinner that maybe can be reheated and we can talk this over. Please, Danny."

The cold calm surrounding Daniel fractured into tiny pieces. Everything was in bright color, once again warm and vibrant. He stepped back and opened the door wide enough for Erik to slip through.

"I do not get cranky when I haven't eaten." Daniel tried to take the bag from him, but Erik moved out of his way.

"Careful, I think it started leaking when I dropped it. The handles snapped when I was running." Erik set the bag carefully down on the table. "You do get cranky when you haven't eaten. And so do I. Two hungry, cranky people should not try to have a rational conversation about anything, so I went and got us takeout. I know I should have told you that's where I was going, but I just—"

"You were running?" Daniel poked in the bag where white cardboard boxes leaked what looked like Kung Pao chicken sauce. His heart warmed. Erik had been running, trying to find him.

"Yeah," Erik said softly. He dropped into the chair opposite Daniel's. "I got back home, and you weren't there and I kind of freaked out."

"Well, what was I supposed to think?" Daniel cleared his plate of macaroni and cheese off the table; it would keep. He smiled at the boxes, opened them and dumped the contents onto plates to be reheated in the microwave. He smiled at the microwave as he closed the door and started it. He was smiling at inanimate objects, but was still somehow too nervous to smile at Erik. He took a deep breath and turned around.

Erik said, "You were supposed to think—you're supposed to know that I love you, and just because we have a disagreement doesn't mean that I don't love you, or want you."

"I love you, too," Daniel said softly.

"I love you so much, Danny. I—please, just stick with me. I know I'm not the easiest person to live with, but please don't go anywhere. I need you."

Throat tight, Daniel was embarrassingly close to tears. This kind of declaration of love happened in books and movies, not to *him*.

"I need you, too. I'm sorry I got all—" Daniel made a whirling motion with his hands. "And I'm sorry that I'm not the easiest person to live with, either."

"I'm sorry I stormed out. I'm probably going to do that from time to time. I need some time to figure out what I am trying to say, and it's hard for me to do that when someone's pushing me to talk before I'm ready. So, I might need to take a break during a disagreement—"

"I'm sorry—"

"Just, please. It doesn't mean I'm leaving you."

"You're going somewhere, but you're not leaving."

"Exactly. I'm never going to *leave* you. I just will need some time alone, okay?"

"I'm never going to *leave* you either." Daniel smiled as Erik's bright blue eyes sparkled at him. *God, how did I ever wind up with a guy like this?* An actual nice guy: a genuinely good person who was smart and funny and cared so much about him?

"Then, will you feed me please? I'm wasting away over here," Erik pleaded, grinning. "I'm so hungry I could eat a moose."

The microwave beeped behind Daniel, and he pulled the plate out. "Sorry, fresh out of moose. Would you find Kung Pao chicken a suitable substitute?" He squinted at the plate. "At least, I think it's Kung Pao chicken."

Erik smiled and got up to get forks for them both. "If you're eating it with me, then yes."

Eight Months Before the Wedding

The message light on Daniel's phone had been blinking since two-thirty that morning. It sat on the table on his side of the bed, innocently charging, as always, but this morning, he hated it. The light blinked in a seventeen-second interval. With Erik at another meeting in Sweden, he'd had plenty of time to count it in his head throughout the night, staring sleeplessly at his ceiling in the dark. At the moment, Daniel couldn't decide what annoyed him more: the light flashing all night, the weird interval at which it flashed, or the messages waiting for him.

Good morning, Daniel!

Here's your friendly weekly planning round-up email from your friends at Aurora! We've compiled the newest comments from your BeStabulous account for easier viewing.

We've noticed it's been a few days since you've checked any items off your checklists. We hope you're not burned out! After you've checked out your messages, why don't you take a break today? Revive and replenish your body and your soul by checking out some of our wellness partners. (Click <u>here</u> for coupons, sales, great deals and more at area *spas, salons and restaurants.) Better yet, take Erik with you, and enjoy some bonding time to connect and kindle some pre-wedding flames!*

What's Trending on Aurora? Sumptuous Cinderella Wedding Fabulous Fad: Dress Your Wedding Party as Pumpkins! Click <u>here</u> to read the article about your next wedding must-have!

Click <u>here</u> to see your new comments from BeStabulous!

"Sometimes you exhaust me, Aurora," he grumbled as he lay back down in bed, holding his phone up over his head. He rubbed at his eyes, which were gritty and tired. His head throbbed.

Daniel, welcome back to BeStabulous, the world's most fabulous idea-gathering website, especially for the world's most fabulous people. Who wants to pin ideas when you can stab them?

Your current BeStabulous comment invitees: AndreJustAndre (Andre Lewis), EweBitchStasia (Stasia Pavlenko), Wildwood-ShepherdessCarynne (Carynne Oleander), TryptometricFilotron (Erik Kappel), UrBabyMama (Kate Thompson), JerryGarcia-Rulz (Stefan Jones), MommyMargie (Margaret Whitcomb), AnnikaAhlgren (Annika Ahlgren). Click here to invite more Stabbers from your contact list.

New BeStabulous comments on: Gothic Luxury reception theme possibility?

WildwoodShepherdessCarynne (1 day ago): very romantic

AndreJustAndre (1 day ago): we could recreate those silver candelabras in ceramics and silver paint, I bet. I'd be happy to help out.

EweBitchStasia: (1 day ago) Are you a fucking vampire?

JerryGarciaRulz: (12h ago) This one has an evil vibe, dude. Don't mean to be a downer, but I definitely vote "no way."

AnnikaAhlgren: (12h ago) This is ridiculous.

(private message from EweBitchStasia: (10h ago) Is -she- a fucking vampire? That would explain a lot.)

MommyMargie: (10h ago) Dear Daniel, This looks exactly like the reception Canyon and Brock had on One World to Turn back in the 1980s and I always thought it was so beautiful and romantic. This was before Canyon found out she was an alien clone carrying Ridge's baby. I hope you and Erik will be happier than they were. Call me later. It's your sister's birthday tomorrow. Love, your mother.

Daniel also found his mother exhausting. She just was... exhausting. He'd given up trying to tell her she didn't need to write every message like a letter from 1952; it was like banging his head against a brick wall. He'd also given up trying to figure out her thought processes while writing the messages. It was as if she just threw darts at random thoughts to include. And besides, what was she doing with her screenname? He'd never called her "Mommy" in his life. He scowled at his phone as he continued to scroll through the messages.

New BeStabulous comments on: Rustic Charm reception ideas— whaddya think?

EweBitchStasia: (2 days ago) No fucking way.

WildwoodShepherdessCarynne: (2 days ago) Stasia don't be so judgmental. This is simple and elegant.

EweBitchStasia: (1 day ago) Mason jar glasses and paper napkins are not elegant. It's trashy as all hell.

JerryGarciaRulz: (19h ago) These colors have a real open aura feel to them. Good times. Relaxed vibes. Could rock.

AndreJustAndre: (14h ago) this looks really affordable

UrBabyMama: (12h ago) I think we can find something classier. I like the candle colors, I like the wildflowers in the buckets, I like the picture frames for the place card holders, though.

AnnikaAhlgren: (12h ago) Cheap, gaudy and provincial

MommyMargie: (12h ago) Dear Daniel, I think Mrs. Johnson has a bunch of checkered tablecloths just like these saved up for the Winnetka Club's blueberry festival. I bet if you called her and asked nicely, she'd let you and Erik borrow them. They probably also have folding chairs and tables to borrow. Also, is Kate really going to be your surrogate, because I heard on the news there was a scandal in New York City about a fertility clinic with shady business dealings. Love, your mother.

TryptometricFilotron: (12h ago) No.

Daniel was annoyed. It was hard enough to plan a wedding when your fiancé was in the same room, and it was next to impossible when he was halfway across the world and leaving completely unhelpful comments on your reception ideas. "No." What kind of a goddamned answer was that? It is not a yes or no proposition. Comments are supposed to be... lengthier and actually give a helpful opinion. Not just, "No."

He swiped to his phone screen, ready to call Erik and share with him exactly how much he enjoyed his long-distance "help" getting their fucking wedding planned. It would be lunchtime in Sweden, and Erik had a day-long meeting with several corporate investors in the archaeology program. He wouldn't be answering his phone right in the middle of it.

Daniel's phone chimed with new message notifications.

New BeStabulous comments on: Rustic Charm, take 2!

AndreJustAndre: (1 day ago) This would be easy to recreate. We could take a camping trip to Green Lake and get everything, if we could get a logging permit.

JerryGarciaRulz: (1 day ago) Lumberjacks are awesome

WildwoodShepherdessCarynne: (1 day ago) It could be nice.

EweBitchStasia: (20h ago) That's a lot of wood. And not the good kind.

UrBabyMama: (8h ago) I like the lights in the branches. I like the birch bark wraps for the tea lights. I think the moss could be problematic - maybe it'd be better with less of it? More like "with moss accents"?

TryptometricFilotron: (3 minutes ago) I like lumberjacks.

Daniel giggled. Goddamned Erik, making him giggle when Daniel was supposed to be annoyed at him. "Lumberjacks" had been their own private joke, ever since their first foray into watching porn together.

For his birthday, a plain-brown-paper-wrapped package had arrived in the mail, and through laughter and shrieks of horror, they drank birthday champagne and watched it. It was cringe-worthy, terrible lighting, awkward dialogue, but it was undeniably hot. The guys in it may not have been great actors, but they definitely were enjoying their other onscreen duties. And it had been definitely enjoyable watching it with his new boyfriend, flushed and squirming and so goddamned hot, himself, on the couch next to him. It became a joke that either of them could just whisper the word "lumberjack" and give the other a Pavlovian erection.

Daniel flushed, remembering. Erik had posted that flippant comment three minutes ago, right in the middle of the meeting. Daniel pictured him straight-faced and dressed in a suit and tie, probably during a break, turning away from his colleagues to type it, maybe shifting in his seat to hide how tight his pants had become.

Should he send Erik a few risqué messages to encourage him? *Oh yes, that might work out quite nicely.*

Instead he sneezed. Once, twice, three times. He squinted one eye, trying to find the Kleenex, and wiped his phone off on his shirt. His head really did ache.

Daniel groaned as he dragged himself out of bed and shuffled his way across the small apartment above Co-Op. He'd painted everything with a heavy-duty paint before he'd moved in: the walls, the woodwork, the ceiling, the floor. The paint covered all sorts of stains, scuffs, bad carpentry and god-knows-what else. He'd chosen a buttery cream color because it was first, cheerful and second, on sale. Just now the paint reflected the sunlight directly in his eyes from all angles, and he hated it. He rummaged in the bathroom cabinet for something for his headache and caught sight of his glassy eyes in the mirror.

He took his temperature: 101.7. It wasn't high enough to be worried, but it was definitely high enough to get him out of having lunch with his family today.

He messaged Carynne that he wouldn't be coming in to the shop. He was getting ready to send Erik a dick pic to keep the rest of his meeting interesting—he was feverish, not dead—and decided against it just as he heard Carynne pounding up the stairs from the store. She brought him a steaming hot mug of Stefan's new Breathe-sy Easy herbal tea. Carynne fussed over getting him tucked back in bed, as he gleefully sent his mother a message saying he was running a fever, and there just wasn't any way he could possibly make it to his sister's birthday lunch.

Two years ago

"Babe, are you here?" Daniel called as he came through the front door, slipping his keys back into his messenger bag so he wouldn't lose them. The deadbolt had been unlocked. Maybe Erik had used his new keys to Daniel's apartment and was waiting for him.

Erik's head popped up over the back of the couch. He looked exhausted. "Yes. I'm here."

"Oh god, babe, what's wrong?"

"I don't know." Erik's eyes glittered feverishly. "My head hurts and my stomach hurts and I—I feel like I might throw up. Maybe it's food poisoning?"

"Oh, honey," Daniel cooed, launching into mothering mode. "You poor thing. Let's get you some ginger ale, and into some more comfortable clothes."

He grabbed Erik's pajama pants and a short-sleeved T-shirt from the pile of unfolded clean laundry in the bedroom. They'd progressed to sharing apartment keys and doing their laundry together, and Daniel couldn't deny the bubble of happiness calm domesticity gave him. He had an urge to take care of Erik, to bake him cookies, fold his socks, smooth his hair when he was disheveled, coo at him when he did something adorable. He also had the urge to fuck him into the mattress, worship his naked body, tie him up and lick him from head to toe and everywhere in between, so it all balanced out. At least, he hoped it balanced out. It was a work in progress.

He hesitated to take care of a sick Erik. He just hoped he wouldn't annoy Erik by going overboard and being too smothering, or motherly or whatever.

When Daniel came back into the living room, Erik was in the bathroom. After a few moments, Erik emerged.

"I thought I was going to puke, so I went in there, just in case." Erik swallowed gingerly. "But, no."

"Oh, you poor thing." Daniel resisted the urge to rush over and help him and let Erik settle himself carefully on the couch.

He went into the bathroom and grabbed a bath towel, picking up the small, empty garbage can on his way to the kitchen, where he rummaged around until he found the roll of garbage bags. He flipped a fresh bag into the can before setting it down next to the couch, where Erik was lying down looking pale and miserable. He dragged over the fan, turned it on low speed and angled it so it was blowing near the couch, but not directly on it.

"Here, love," Daniel murmured. "You stand up and put your PJs on, and I'll put this towel down. That way, you don't have to make it to the bathroom before you throw up."

"I really don't want to throw up in front of you." Erik's voice was muffled as he shrugged into his sleep shirt.

"Babe, intimacy is not always about romance." Daniel went to the kitchen and found a dusty can of ginger ale hidden on the back of a shelf.

"Still." Erik lay back down with a groan. "I don't want to."

"I know you don't want to. Nobody wants to throw up, not really." Daniel poured the ginger ale into a glass and set that down on the coffee table in front of Erik. "I'm going to go make a supply run to the store for more ginger ale and some straws for you to drink out of, and some other things. Is there anything that might taste good to you, or anything you want?"

"Crackers, maybe?" Erik grimaced. "I don't know, I don't really want to think about food right now."

"It's okay." Daniel smiled encouragingly. "Can I put a movie on?"

"Sure." Erik smiled back at him. "You could just start whatever's in the DVD player."

"Sure thing, love." Daniel pressed "play" on the machine and navigated through the menus, and *The Avengers* began. "I'm going to run out right now, but I'll be back as soon as I can, okay? You'll be okay here until I get back?"

"Mm-hm."

Daniel shoved his shoes on and trotted down the stairs and into the sticky, sweltering heat of a July evening in Tallenburg. The new grocery store just up the block was small but it had the basics he'd need. He sped through the store, dropping things into his basket as he tried to think about what Erik might like or need while he was sick, not knowing how long Erik might be ill: two twelve-packs of ginger ale in cans, a bag of cheerfully bright drinking straws, some crackers, some herbal tea, a few apples and some rice. He hurriedly paid for everything, shoved it all into bags and rushed back home.

As he unlocked the door, he could hear the toilet flush. The bathroom door opened, and Erik stood there, pale and trembling.

"I threw up," he said, clearly on the verge of tears.

"Oh, honey, I'm sorry," Daniel said as he put the groceries down and went to help Erik shuffle back to the couch. "Would you be more comfortable in bed?"

"No." Erik shook his head slowly. "I'm so sorry for throwing up in your apartment."

"Oh, baby, it's not like you threw up all over the apartment. You threw up in the bathroom. It's okay," he soothed. "And it's not really *my* apartment anymore, right? We're sharing it, right?"

"Because my apartment is—"

"In the middle of a college dorm and neither one of us can really bear to be there." Daniel helped Erik back to the couch. "Plus, we're in love and I love having you in my bed—our bed— every night. I don't sleep well without you."

Erik smiled. "Would you... would you come sit with me? Just for a little bit?"

"Of course, love." Daniel had never seen Erik so helpless and needy— needing *him*—and his heart clenched a little bit.

"And could I maybe put my head in your lap?" Erik asked quietly.

"Oh, love, of course." Daniel settled on the couch, leaned back a bit and chuckled when Erik didn't put his head down on his thigh, but crept into his arms and lay down next to him. Daniel could feel Erik's fever hot through his shirt, and the slight tremor that was running through him. He gave in to his instinct and gently ran his head through Erik's hair; he was gratified when Erik sighed and relaxed farther into him.

Daniel propped his feet up on the coffee table and nestled into the couch to get more comfortable. Erik dozed, sometimes snoring softly, while Daniel watched the rest of the movie. When it ended, Daniel gingerly tried to maneuver the remote closer with his foot so he could turn the television off without disturbing Erik. It didn't work. He had to shift his whole body, stretch his arm out and scrabble for it with his fingertips.

Erik jolted slightly, waking just enough to murmur, "Please, Danny. Don't go anywhere."

Daniel's heart actually ached. It was cheesy, but true. It was terrible that Erik was so sick, but Daniel was ridiculously happy at this proof that Erik wanted him around, that he actually needed him. Erik was so independent and strong, usually. Even though Erik had told Daniel he needed him when they had their first big fight, it was nice to *feel* needed.

"Of course, love," he whispered into Erik's hair. "I just need to get up for a minute, but I'll come right back."

"Mmm." Erik nodded.

Daniel was worried at how quickly Erik seemed to fall asleep. Erik probably couldn't keep anything down, at least not yet. Daniel wet a washcloth with cool water to put on Erik's forehead. He got himself a drink and a snack, changed DVDs and tried to climb back under Erik's torso. Halfway through the next movie, Erik sat up abruptly and bolted for the bathroom, where he was noisily and violently sick.

Daniel got him a glass of water and waited outside the bathroom door until Erik emerged. Erik's face was pale and covered in a sheen of sweat.

Daniel handed him the glass. "Just sip it, okay?"

"I'm sorry, Danny," Erik said between tiny sips.

"Oh, stop. You don't have anything to be sorry for."

"I just hate throwing up."

"I know, love. Let's get you back to the couch."

Erik's phone rang a few minutes later. When Eric could manage only vague grunts and hand gestures, Daniel answered it.

It was Antonio, checking in on Erik.

"Dr. Smithson called in to say he and his son were in the emergency room with severe dehydration because they've been so sick. Apparently, there's a particularly virulent stomach thing going around," Antonio explained. "A bit of an epidemic, I gather."

"Yeah." Daniel glanced at Erik lying on the couch. "I think he's really feeling awful."

"And Dr. Martin said he wasn't feeling well either," Antonio continued. "And neither am I. I think the entire department is going to be sick with it."

"Oh god."

"Yes. If I were you, Daniel, I would be washing my hands like crazy and doing anything I could not to get it."

"Oh god, I'll try."

They hung up a few moments later. Daniel did his best to ignore the strange cramping feeling in his stomach as he sat back down. He'd drunk too much soda at lunch. Or it was just the power of suggestion? He was freaking out about getting sick, so he felt as though he was getting sick. It was nothing.

Halfway through the next movie, though, he had to bolt to the bathroom himself.

"I'm so sorry, Danny," Erik called through the bathroom door.

"Listen, you idiot, go lie down before you fall over." Daniel grimaced as his stomach tried to turn itself inside out again.

They spent the better part of the next two days alternating turns in the bathroom, each one trying manfully to keep from being sick so the other could use it.

"We're ridiculous, you know that, right?" After much protesting from Erik, Daniel had put his yoga mat down, then made a nest of blankets and pillows on the living room floor. "We're like Mr. Darcy or something, arguing with himself."

"No, no, after you, my good man," Erik murmured, his arm flung over his eyes. "I insist."

"Jolly good." Daniel chuckled weakly. "Right-o."

"Do you need any more Powerade?" Erik lifted his head to peer at him. "Or crackers or anything?"

"I've still got some, thanks," Daniel said as he reached blindly for his cup. He sipped carefully through his straw. "You?"

"No, I'm good." Erik lay back down. "I haven't thrown up in three hours. Maybe I'm on way back to normal?"

"Oh, I hope so."

Erik got up and shuffled toward the DVD player to change the disc. "We need more DVDs."

"Yeah," Daniel agreed. "And, I just want to say—"

"Yes?" Erik smiled at him as he walked back to the couch, scruffy-faced, pale and worn out.

"If I had to be puking my guts out, I'm really glad I've been doing it with you."

"Yeah." Erik's smiled widened. "Me, too. I'm fucking miserable, but less miserable with you."

Eight Months Before the Wedding

Good morning, Daniel!

Congratulations on choosing your photographer! 22 new items have been added to your checklist. (<u>Choose ceremony readings</u>. <u>Define ceremony space dimensions and layout</u>. <u>Coordinate bridal party mani-pedi outing</u>. <u>Click here for more.</u>)

New BeStabulous comments on: Unexpected pairings - Kale and cabbage floral arrangements, table toppers, boutonnieres, corsages and topiary installations

EweBitchStasia: (3 days ago) Are we fucking rabbits?

JerryGarciaRulz: (3 days ago) they're fucking -like- rabbits, am I right, Danny?

EweBitchStasia: (3 days ago) Stefan, don't ever speak to me ever again. I really mean it, this time.

AndreJustAndre: (1 day ago) That -is- a very unexpected pairing. I think these table toppers are okay, I think the floral arrangements work. I'm not sure about cabbage in the boutonnieres and corsages.

WildwoodShepherdessCarynne: (1 day ago) This is such a great idea, Danny! Not only are they beautiful, but at the end of the reception, you could boil them all down and make a really lovely and healthy soup stock. You could also go completely organic.

UrBabyMama: (19 hours ago) I don't understand. What the fuck is a topiary installation?

AnnikaAhlgren: (5 hours ago) No.

MommyMargie: (5 minutes ago) Dear Daniel, Mrs. Schultz has a bunch of cabbages in her garden. She was going to make sauerkraut with them but I'm pretty sure we could have some of them. Also, we're painting the living room. Do you think blue would look good in there? Love, your mother.

New BeStabulous comments on: Classic 'Father Of The Bride' movie magic reception ideas

AndreJustAndre: (2 days ago) This looks really classy

UrBabyMama: (1 day ago) SUCH A GOOD MOVIE!!

MommyMargie: (1 minute ago) Dear Daniel, this looks lovely. You've always loved this movie and do you remember when you used to pretend to be marrying Elizabeth Taylor? Your father has a video of it somewhere. But, which one of you is the bride? Love, your mother.

Clearly, Daniel was going to have to have another conversation with his mother, about… everything. He thought he'd done a pretty good job explaining his life over the years, explaining how neither he nor his partner were "the woman," showing his parents how they were locked in heteronormative thinking. He was so tired of thinking he needed to be The Gay, the poster boy for all things gay, having to educate and re-educate his family over and over. It's as if they only half-listened and didn't internalize any of it.

He sneezed four times in a row, wiped his nose and tossed his phone across the bed. He would have a talk with his mother, he would. Just, not right now.

"ERIK, YOU SEXY MOTHERFUCKER, HOW are you?" Stasia hung her leather jacket on the coatrack, kicked off her motorcycle boots and padded barefoot into Erik and Daniel's living room. She knelt on the couch next to Erik and gave him a kiss on each cheek—their usual greeting.

"Hi, *liebchen*." He smiled at her, using a German diminutive nickname his mother used. She was so small, he couldn't help himself. "I'm fine. Ooh, you smell good, what's new with you?"

"No ciggies for three weeks now," she announced.

"That's amazing! Are you wearing the patch, or chewing gum, or what?"

"None of that." With a sigh of contentment, she slid to sit next to him. "I met a girl and I'm in love."

"Oh my god, what happened to Patrick?" Stasia and Patrick had been dating for several years.

"He's fine, we're still together. We're both in love with Indira."

"Indira, huh?" Erik grinned at her. "Tell me about her. Would I approve of her?"

"Oh, she's amazing. She's smart and she's funny, and she's really into community activism and—"

"And she doesn't like smoking," Erik interrupted.

"Bingo. She says she won't kiss a smoker, and fuck me, I will do *anything* for a taste of that sweet—"

"Ah! La la la la. None of that kind of talk!" Daniel came out of the bedroom with a huge stack of folders and headed into the kitchen. "We don't talk about our sex life to you; we don't hear about yours."

"Why is Groomzilla over there always such a prude?" she mock-whispered to Erik.

"I heard that!" Daniel called.

Erik leaned toward her. "Trust me, he's not always such a prude."

"I'm glad he's got some hidden talents in the bedroom because sometimes I just do not see how you put up with him."

Erik chuckled. "He's got other talents, too. But sometimes, I do want to bop him with one of those cartoon hammers, you know?"

"Oh my god, I know that feeling."

"I heard that, too!" Daniel yelled, coming back into the living room. "Groomzilla is here to inform you, Stasia, that Annika will be arriving any moment."

Stasia hissed and made her fingers into a cross. "You didn't tell me about Vampira being here, Danny. I didn't bring my garlic or my stakes."

"Be nice," Erik admonished. "She's one of my oldest friends."

"And this is how I knew you were a good man," Stasia said as she stood up. "You're always her friend, sticking up for her, even when she's the fucking Ice Princess of Evil."

Erik smiled. This was a conversation he and Daniel had had many times, and he didn't want to hash it all out again. Annika was his friend, probably the woman he loved most in the world aside from his mother and his sister. She did have some sharp edges around people she didn't know very well, but she had let him inside all of that. He knew the real Annika, beneath all the biting comments and chilliness.

"I think she's in love with you," Stasia stated. "I think this is a very sad case of straight woman desperately in love with gay man, and it's eating her up inside and *that's* why she's so awful to everyone."

"Oh, really? Well, thank you, Dr. Stasia for that insightful diagnosis," Daniel quipped, with a sharp look at Erik. "Come on, let's get set up in the kitchen before she gets here and you cause more problems."

"I don't cause problems," she objected, as Daniel took her by both shoulders, spun her around and pushed her towards the kitchen.

Erik caught Daniel's backward glance, and smiled gratefully at him. Daniel smiled ruefully at him—Daniel understood. With all the frustrations they'd been having lately, he was grateful Daniel always understood him.

Daniel hadn't ever warmed to Annika, not that Annika had ever given him the chance. He and Daniel had talked about it, about how much Erik worried that Annika really was in love with him, about how he could never talk to her about it because he was afraid it would break her completely.

He scowled at his reflection in the laptop screen on his lap. He worried he was being self-centered. Maybe he really should confront her about it and force her to move on, to find someone she could actually take a chance on, and actually be in love with and be loved back in the way she needed.

It all came down to all the different ways of loving, and Stasia was a perfect example of that. She didn't love her boyfriend any less because of falling in love with another woman. Her boyfriend didn't love her any less because she had, either. Erik loved Annika very much, was attracted to her wit and her laughter and her steadfastness. She'd been an integral part of him since they were both fifteen years old. Even though he also knew he wasn't *in* love with her, the thought of pushing her out of his life was unimaginable.

He stopped himself. Sometimes, his mind slipped downward and became a Wagnerian opera, all blood and darkness and Valkyries singing arias in front of funeral pyres. He blamed his German heritage and knew his German mother would be chuckling at him. *You can't help the way you feel, darling.*

He pulled himself back to the task at hand—logic, and reason and flowcharts. That's what he needed to concentrate on, that's what he needed to work on. The anthropology department's donors' annual meeting was coming up, and he and Annika had been given the task of creating the after-dinner presentation, which would showcase the accomplishments of the year and their continued need for funding.

The buzzer at the front door of the building sounded. Annika had arrived.

THE KITCHEN TABLE SQUEAKED AS Stasia plunked herself down at it, dropped her bag on the floor and grabbed her latest knitting project from it.

"I'm sorry you fuckers are so fucking gigantic that you can't even have normal-sized chairs." She dragged another chair closer to her and put her feet up on it.

"Dude, those are normal-sized chairs." Daniel teased. "I'm sorry you're so fucking short your feet don't reach the ground."

"Hey, hey," she protested. "My feet reach the ground, okay? They just don't reach the ground *very well.*"

Erik chuckled. Annika had pulled out her own laptop, and they were busy finding appropriate departmental photographs to add to the presentation.

"Okay, so, question of the hour is: flower girl or no flower girl?" Daniel asked.

"Vote 'no,' Stasia!" Erik hollered from his perch on the couch.

"Hey, you're supposed to be busy out there," Daniel teased him. "I'm in here discussing this with my Matron of Bitch."

"Fuck you, I'm not a matron," Stasia began to knit.

"Fuck you, you are, too. Patrick is your common-law husband, and that makes you married, and that makes you a matron."

Stasia grimaced. "That makes me sound dumpy as a potato and old. What am I, a prison guard or something?"

"Would you rather be my "Maid"?

"Fuck you, no, I wouldn't." Stasia scowled. "And I vote no flower girl. Flower girls get stuck in a floofy stupid dress and she'll feel stupid. And floofy."

"But Carynne's daughter as a flower girl. Without the floofy dress."

"Oh, that *would* be adorable.

"Yeah." Daniel leaned on the kitchen counter. "She's *adorable.* She's four years old. She'll be perfect as a flower girl!"

"Okay, well, maybe." With a whoop of triumph, Stasia cast off the final stitches of the shawl she'd been knitting to sell at Co-Op. She folded it in and put it carefully in her bag. "I'm listening."

"So, she's cute, she's adorable, she walks down the aisle, she throws the flower petals," Daniel listed off happily. "It'll be adorable."

"Are you going to make her stand up there the whole ceremony? Or are you going to dragoon Carynne into making her behave?"

"I've already thought of that. My cousin, Maggie, had the best idea. You put a coin down on the floor and you tell the flower girl she can have it, but only if she stands on the coin the whole time."

"Capitalist wedding/industrial complex, at its finest." Stasia started casting on a new project. "What coin are you going to use? A nickel?"

"I think she's too smart for that, and she'll realize that a nickel isn't worth standing still for so long. We've got to go bigger."

"A Susan B. Anthony dollar!" Stasia exclaimed. "Feminist icon, right there."

"Or you could use a Sacajawea dollar," Annika offered, still working on her laptop. Erik looked at her in surprise. Usually, she avoided all of their wedding discussions like the plague.

"Oh, Sacajawea, another feminist icon." Stasia nodded. "Now, you've just got to choose between them."

"With Sacajawea, you'd also be including Native American icons in your ceremony." Annika added.

To Erik's amazement, Stasia and Annika began debating the coin choice as if it were a court case, calmly and solemnly. Daniel and Stasia came into the living room, so they could talk more freely.

"But the Susan B. Anthony dollar is silver colored, and Danny's been working on gold tones with the flowers. It'll clash!" Stasia asserted.

"It's on the floor, no one will see it." Annika sniffed dismissively. "Plus, the child will be standing on it."

"Good point," Stasia agreed.

Looking astonished, Daniel gingerly sat down on the couch next to Erik.

"A: They're not ripping each other's heads off, and b: they're actually discussing this like it's a big deal. And c: they're not ripping each other's heads off!" Daniel whispered. "What the hell is going on here?"

Erik whispered back, "I don't know. But I'm afraid to disturb them. I'm afraid they'll start eating each other or something."

"But, really, you have to think about the precedent being set," Annika said. "Standing on the head of a woman, even in symbolic form. Is that really the message we want to send?"

"Oh, that's a good point," Stasia agreed.

"So, which coin do we have the child stand on?" Annika asked.

"I think it's got bad vibes to have her stand on the coin of a serial adulterer like JFK, though he did make important strides in many areas. Honoring dishonesty is not the way to begin a marriage."

"Oh, my god," Daniel whispered. "They're still at it. Why are they still talking about this?"

Erik chuckled and slid his hand into Daniel's. "Do you really want to have a flower girl in our wedding? Like, really?"

"No, it was just an idea I was throwing out there. I didn't really expect this massive discussion about it."

The flower girl debate turned to what alternatives to coins a four-year-old might value and the morality of bribing a four-year-old to good behavior.

"Then we're agreed, no flower girl?" Erik whispered.

"Agreed." Daniel leaned his head on Erik's shoulder. "But let's not tell them until later. Maybe when they're separate. I don't want them to eat *us.*"

"Yeah, I know what you mean." Erik chortled. "We'll just sit here—no sudden movements—and wait for a pause."

"I'll bring some wine in. They'll go for that, and then we can regroup and get them back to work."

"An excellent plan, love. Do you need any help with that?"

"Not really, but if you'd like to accompany me to the kitchen, I'm sure I could help *you* with something."

"Oh god, yes," Erik stood quickly and pulled Daniel up off the couch.

"Oh, no. No, no, no," Stasia shouted. "The boys are going to go sneak off to the kitchen for some hanky-panky fooling around. I know those faces you're making and I have walked in on that shit enough times to know better."

"We're just going to get some wine," Daniel protested.

"You're just going to *get some,*" Stasia retorted genially. "Just ease up on the slurping sounds, 'kay? Annika and I are making some real progress out here."

"Chardonnay as usual, Annika?" Erik turned to ask her, still smiling.

"Thanks, Erik, yes."

"You heard the lady, Daniel," Erik teased. "We've got some making out to do in the kitchen. Let's get on that."

THREE YEARS AGO

It was their first dinner with Daniel's extended family, at a restaurant near Daniel's apartment, and it was clear Daniel was about to lose it. He'd changed his shirt three times and his pants twice and dithered for over an hour about what tie to wear and then decided to wear a nice sweater instead.

"I don't understand why you're so frantic right now." Erik grabbed Daniel by the waist and wrapped his arms around him. "I mean, I know you don't really get along with your mother, but the rest of them, they're your family."

"Yes, of course, they love me," Daniel squirmed in Erik's arms, craning his neck to try to choose one of the sweaters spread out on the bed. "Of course they do."

"Then why are you so worked up?"

"They're just—you'll see."

At the restaurant, Daniel's mother began clucking fretfully over the length of Daniel's hair and picking invisible lint from the arm of his sweater. As the waitress brought the appetizers they'd ordered, Erik's face turned redder and redder, as if his blood were beginning to boil.

Daniel's family was deferential to Erik, as if slightly in awe of him, and yet, as usual, they were already pecking holes in Daniel as if they were determined to tear him down right before Erik's eyes. Was it some strange protective instinct, their determination to protect him by trying to scare off potential suitors before he could become too invested in the relationship?

"And have you been to see his little store, yet?" Daniel's mother leaned across the table at the end of the meal, while everyone else was ordering dessert. "The Coop?"

"I believe it's called 'Co-Op.' And yes. I've been there." Erik smiled tightly.

"Can you believe a college-educated person spends their time there?" The look on Daniel's mother's face clearly indicated she expected Erik to agree with her. "All the hippies back in my day didn't need a store to do their macramé and take their drugs."

"They're building a wonderful and supportive creative community," Erik replied. "And Daniel obviously thrives there."

"All that yarn and the crazy marijuana cupcakes and the jewelry made out of spoons." Daniel's mother shook her head. "I suppose it appeals to a *certain* clientele."

"Mom, there are no marijuana cupcakes. That was Thai basil." Daniel said. "How many times do I have to tell you?"

"Oh, sure, Daniel," his mother said, sarcastically. "I'm sure you'd never admit to your mother you were making marijuana cupcakes."

Erik took a large gulp of water.

"And, you, Erik," Daniel's mother continued. "Daniel tells us you're teaching at the university, right?"

"Yes. I'm actually doing graduate studies there, but I do teach a few classes."

"And you're here permanently, or do you have to go back to Europe soon?"

"I'm here for at least the next year." He smiled politely. "Where and how I'm going to complete my research will determine when I'll be going back to Sweden."

"And are you from Sweden?" she asked, smiling blankly.

"Germany, actually."

"Oh. But you don't look German." She frowned, looking puzzled.

"Mom, not all Germans have blond hair and blue eyes." Daniel sounded exasperated.

"Well, it looks like Daniel's certainly happy to be with you, Erik," Daniel's mother said. "Isn't that what they say? Happiness makes you fat?"

Daniel's face flushed.

"I mean, he's always been such a skinny thing, so gawky and awkward. You'd never believe how skinny he was, Erik. So skinny. He used to take after *my* side of the family."

Daniel bit his lip and tore his paper napkin into tiny shreds. Erik looked at him, but if he caught Erik's eye, Daniel wouldn't be able to keep control over his face.

"Daniel's just so lucky to have met someone like you." Daniel's mother nearly tipped over her wine glass.

"I'm so lucky to have Daniel, too," Erik said.

"Oh, isn't that romantic?" Daniel's mother sighed.

"You know, it's just so surprising that Danny found such a good-looking guy like you," Daniel's cousin said with a smile plastered on her face. "I'd read in *Cosmo* that there was real pressure within the gay community to be, you know, physically fit and hot and attractive, and that got me really, really worried he'd never be able to find someone."

Erik wiped his lips fiercely with his napkin, "I'm sorry, but I can't continue this anymore. This is just... unbelievable to me."

He stood and glared directly at every person at the table in turn. "You should be ashamed of yourselves. You say you love Daniel, you say you support him, and yet, so far today, you've done nothing but tear him down. Not a single one of you has had anything positive to say about Daniel. I can't believe you people."

"Now see here—" Daniel's uncle began.

Erik dropped his napkin on his plate. "I'm not going to sit here and listen to you amuse yourselves by ripping him apart and saying it's love. It's not love, it's bullying."

"Erik—" Daniel started.

"Danny, you don't have to sit here and take this. Why do you sit here and take this?"

Daniel looked around the table, at the shocked and angry faces of his family. "Erik, I—"

"Please, Danny, I can't bear how they treat you. Please come with me."

Chilled and vaguely nauseated, Daniel felt his nerves spark all over his body. Part of him wanted to smooth it all over. This was just how his family *was*, they didn't mean anything by it; they just gave everyone a hard time. *Except my sister, and my cousin and my other cousin,* a tiny insistent voice in his head pointed out. Another part of him was aghast, yet delighted that someone was standing up for him, someone was telling him he was worth more than his family thought. He was worth more than this.

Daniel grinned and stood up so fast his chair lurched back and fell. "I—yeah. I'm coming, too."

As they walked away, Daniel could hear his family whisper and murmur behind them, already gossiping away. Erik took his hand firmly and marched them to the door of the restaurant.

"That was amazing." Daniel giggled when they got outside. "That was just fucking amazing. My aunt Jackie will never speak to me again. I'm free!"

He let go of Erik's hand and did a little dance down the deserted sidewalk, bellowing "Freedom!"

When Erik didn't laugh, Daniel turned around. "Are you okay?"

"I just—I can't believe your family."

"Well. Believe it. That's them, on their best behavior."

"At first, I was thinking that they were just trying to protect you, but by portraying you in the worst possible light? That didn't make any sense? Why would they do that?"

"I don't know." Daniel frowned, a bit baffled at Erik's reaction. "That's pretty much how they are—"

"They're ridiculous!" Erik shouted. "And awful!"

Daniel smiled ruefully. "Mostly, yes. I mean, sometimes they *do* have their nice moments, but—"

"They're mean and horrible, Danny. I can't believe they can't see you. I can't believe they can't see how wonderful you are."

Goose bumps sprang up all over Daniel's body. Erik's way of telling him his feelings, point-blank and without reservation, made him feel sparkling and bubbling inside.

"How can they not see how funny you are?" Erik shouted. "You're the funniest, sweetest, kindest, best man I've ever met, and how *dare* they have you in their midst and not acknowledge it? They're lucky to have you, Danny. How dare they try to make you feel bad about yourself, when you're so amazing?"

"Why are you yelling right now?"

"I'm yelling because I love you so much that I can't even take it. I love you so much I can't bear the thought of anyone making you feel bad about yourself. I don't know how to handle it. I love you, Danny."

Daniel wasn't sure what to say or what to think. His stomach flip-flopped and his hands were cold and shaky, but the rush of happiness running through him brought a ridiculous grin to his face.

"You love me?"

"I—yeah, Danny." Erik chuckled, all the fire rushing out of him. "I do. I love you, I can't—I can't *not* tell you that any more. I can't hold it in any more."

There was a lump in his throat, a tightening in his chest, and he was pretty sure he was about to cry. "I love you, too."

Erik laughed, grabbing Daniel's hand and pulling him close. "I'm sorry."

"For what?"

"For offending your entire family and then yelling at you about how wonderful you are and how much I love you."

"The offending my entire family thing is okay by me. I mean, Christmas with them is going to be awful no matter what we do, so we might as well do what we need to do, you know?"

Erik kissed him on the nose.

"But, next time, you can just *tell* me how much you love me and how wonderful I am, okay? No need to bellow. I can hear you just fine."

"I wasn't bellowing—"

"—Were, too." Daniel smiled.

"God, I love you." Erik laughed.

"Then let's get home and discuss this properly. Preferably naked."

Seven Months Before the Wedding

Good morning, Daniel!

Congratulations on setting your date and reserving your venue! Good work! Your calendar entry is saved! Seven new items have been added to your checklist. (_Throw engagement party_: 42 sub-checklist items. _Plan honeymoon_: 97 sub-checklist items. _Book your officiant_. _Reception table linens color selection_. _Click here for more_.)

Click _here_ to add or modify list entries. Showing 1-6 out of 70 checklist entries left to complete.

What's Trending on Aurora? Ambient Sound Art: Chimes, Bells and Gongs for Your Ceremony Arrival Spaces. Click _here_ to read the article about your next wedding must-have!

Have a great day, Daniel!

Love,
Aurora

"BUT WE CAN'T INVITE ANYONE to the engagement party unless they're going to be invited to the wedding." It was Tuesday Night Spaghetti Night, and Daniel and Erik were cooking together.

"That's a stupid rule." Erik grimaced, dicing onions for pasta sauce.

"Well, I didn't make it up!" Daniel opened the jar of tomato puree and set it on the counter. "That's just what all the books and magazines say."

"So, first, we need a wedding guest list."

"Right." Daniel pulled lettuce out of the fridge and rinsed it. "Gah, I don't even want to do that. My family is ridiculously big. How can I choose who gets to come and who doesn't? And all my half of the invites will go to my family, so I won't get to invite any friends. I mean, I hate Great-aunt Gertrude, but if I don't invite her, I will seriously never hear the end of it. And if I don't invite Mrs. Parkinson, I will *also* seriously never hear the end of it."

"So don't invite Mrs. Parkinson. Who the hell is she anyway?"

"She's lived next door to my grandmother for forty-five years. She's basically family. We will never hear the end of it if we don't invite her. They'll bring it up at every single family party. You know they will."

"That's ridiculous, Danny. This is *our* day. We should get to do what *we* want."

"Try telling that to my family," Daniel muttered as he dropped the washed greens into the spinner and spun it.

"Okay, I will. We are not inviting Mrs. Parkinson or Great-aunt Gertrude or anyone else we can't stand."

"I don't want make any waves—" He ripped the lettuce into pieces and dropped them in the salad bowl.

"It's our wedding, Danny. It's *ours*. We get the final decision."

"Great-aunt Gertrude will have a stroke if she doesn't get an invitation."

"If she's wound up enough to have a stroke for not getting an invitation, she'll have a stroke for some other reason just as well."

"Mmm," Daniel hummed as he cut carrots for the salad.

"It's not our job to make sure we live our lives in such a manner that Great-aunt Gertrude won't have a stroke."

Daniel sighed. "I know."

"Listen, what if we just make a list of everyone we could possibly want to invite, and then we can whittle it down to however many we have budgeted?"

"But you and I both know that if we leave somebody out, we will never hear the end of it from my family."

"Danny—"

"And it won't be in a friendly way, or really in anyway that we'll be able to get mad about. Just little stabs, little reminders of how we've disappointed them—"

"Danny—"

"'Oh, it would have just made Mrs. Whatsherface so happy to see you on your wedding day just one last time before she died.'" Daniel pitched his voice higher, imitating his mother, and swiped the carrots into the salad bowl with his knife. "'When you were four, she made you that crocheted teddy bear you were terrified of that you still haven't sent her a thank-you note for.'"

"Oh god, they would not." Erik chuckled.

"Have you met my family? Of course they would."

Erik drained the pasta as Daniel finished the salad.

"I just want one thing in my life that they can't harp on me about. I just want one thing in my life where they say, 'Wow, that was incredible, Daniel; what a great job.' Just one thing that they can't pick at me about. I'm so tired of being their resident fuck-up, you know?"

"You're not a fuck-up, Danny. You're not. You're incredibly talented and creative and a loving person. A *good* person. You're not a fuck-up."

Daniel sniffed. He wasn't tearing up; he really wasn't. It was the onions. "Yeah," he said quietly. "I'm starting to believe that."

📱

ONE YEAR AGO

"Oh, my god." Erik sat on Daniel's couch, working on his laptop, with his ankles crossed and propped up on the coffee table. It was a Thursday morning, before Daniel was to go into Co-Op for inventory. Erik didn't have any classes all day.

"What?" Daniel asked. He was putting together his sketches and unsuccessfully searching for that new set of pencils he'd bought the other day and stashed in a presumably "safe place."

Erik remained silent, frowning at his computer. Shaking his head as if in disbelief, he continued to read.

"What?" Daniel repeated.

Erik looked up. "It's an email from my friend, Andreas. You remember Andreas?"

"Big, tall, blond hulking Viking-type?"

Erik waggled his head back and forth, considering. "Maybe big, rather tall, and, yes, very blond."

"You realize that describes most of your friends."

Erik smiled briefly and shrugged.

"But you're right about the Viking part. He's from Hannover," he said, as if that explained everything.

One of these days, Daniel was going to have to research German history and find out what all of Erik's strange comments were about.

"What's wrong with maybe-big, rather-tall, yes-very-blond Andreas?"

"He got hit by a bus."

"Oh, my god."

"Yes. Not *too* seriously injured, thankfully, but the hospital in Atlanta refused to let his boyfriend in to see him—"

"Christ."

"And he'd only heard Andreas was injured because the hospital had contacted Andreas' mother, and *she* called Joe to tell him."

"What kind of a fucked-up hospital is this?"

"A very fucked-up one." Erik shifted on the couch. "After Joe got their lawyer involved, the hospital tried to backpedal and said they couldn't "legally" allow anyone in to see him other than his next of kin or immediate family."

"Oh, that's just bullshit."

"Really, the problem is that one of the nurses apparently used several homophobic words to express her opinion of Joe's request."

"Discrimination lawsuit, coming right up." Daniel said, shaking his head. "Sue their asses for millions of dollars."

"Yes," Erik agreed. "They are already doing so, and it seems the hospital is eager to settle out of court for a large sum of money."

"Good. We need to fight injustice and bigotry and bastards like that."

Erik smiled. "They're going to use the settlement to pay for their wedding and go on a honeymoon."

"They're getting married?" Daniel had long since given up any ideas of settling down in the suburbs and raising 2.5 kids and a dog. Too domestic. Too tame. Too boring. That life might be okay for some guys, but not him. He just wasn't "that guy," not anymore. He repeated it so often he almost believed it was true.

"I don't know what I'd do if you were hurt or sick or something, and they wouldn't let me see you." With a resigned sigh, Daniel gave up looking for the pencils and zipped up his bag. "I mean, it would almost be worth the hassle of getting married to make sure shit like that didn't happen."

"Yes. I agree," Erik said, staring at his computer again.

My very own absent-minded professor, Daniel thought and kissed him on the forehead on his way to the kitchen to pack his lunch. Peanut butter and strawberry jelly. *Or maybe I have time to make tuna fish? Do we have any mayo?*

"What do you think about June?" Erik called.

"June?" Daniel replied, his head buried in the cupboard, rummaging. "It's a nice month. Not-too-hot, but warm enough. Lots of sun."

"No, idiot." Erik snorted. "To get married in. You and me."

Daniel nearly dropped the bag of chips he was holding. Did he just get proposed to without knowing about it?

"I—" He struggled to find words. He'd trained himself not to think like this. The guys he dated before, they weren't the marrying kind.

"Daniel?" Erik watched him intently.

But Erik wasn't like any of the other guys he'd dated. Erik was calm and quiet and preferred to stay at home. He was sweet and weird and fun and oddly thoughtful. Daniel pulled the jar of good mayo Erik must have bought for him out of the cupboard and gripped it to keep it from slipping from his suddenly shaking hands.

"You, you're sure? You want to marry me?"

"I've been thinking about it for a while."

"You've been thinking about it for a while," Daniel repeated. He'd thought they were happy, that they were a good fit for each other. But this? It was so soon, so sudden.

"It makes sense," Erik continued. "The tax benefits. If we buy an apartment or house together, the legal implications could be an asset. To say nothing of power of attorney and survivor's benefits, in case anything should happen to either of us."

"Well, you don't need it to get citizenship." Daniel sat down roughly in one of the chairs next to the tiny kitchen table.

"No, not with an American father. I got mine when I was born." Erik set his computer down on the coffee table and turned to look at Daniel steadily.

Daniel smiled ruefully. "This isn't exactly how I'd pictured this going."

"You'd pictured a romantic proposal, I know. Danny, come here and sit with me, please?"

Daniel sat next to Erik on the couch and tucked himself in as Erik wrapped his arm around his shoulder and pulled him close.

"I've been thinking about it for a while now, yes. I've known I want to spend the rest of my life with you for a long time now, but I didn't see any reason to rush things. We've got the rest of our lives together."

"May I suggest that next time you propose to me, you lead with that part and leave the potential tax benefits until later." Daniel laughed, though his eyes were teary. He toyed with the button on Erik's flannel shirt. "Also, when things come up like you realize you want to spend the rest of your life with me—you should feel free to share those kinds of things as they happen."

"Okay." Erik took Daniel's other hand and began softly playing with his fingers. "I'm sorry I didn't share it as soon as I realized it."

"It's okay. You shared it, eventually." Daniel grinned. "I mean, it's weird and crazy and sudden, but it's good."

"And I'm sorry this wasn't a more romantic proposal." Erik took hold of one of Daniel's hands, playing gently with his fingers.

"Oh, it was fine," Daniel scoffed.

"You'd pictured maybe a proposal, in front of the crowds, on one of the scoreboards at a baseball game."

Daniel choked back a laugh. "How did you know that?"

"Danny, I *know* you. But you hate baseball. How was I supposed to get you to agree to go to a baseball game?"

"True." Daniel said dreamily. "I would have put up a fuss about going to a baseball game."

"I thought about having the puppy bring you some sort of note, maybe somehow attach the ring to her collar."

"What puppy?"

"The puppy I was going to get—we're ready for a dog, aren't we?"

"An engagement puppy?" Daniel grinned. "So far, I like that proposal idea the best. We are *so* ready for a puppy."

Erik hummed his agreement, kissing Daniel's forehead.

"Underneath that serious college professor exterior, you're really a romantic at heart." Daniel twisted in Erik's arms to lay partially across Erik's lap, then kissed him. Work could wait. It wasn't every day a boy got engaged.

"Don't tell anyone. You'll ruin my reputation." Erik kissed him again, long and slow and exactly as Daniel liked it.

Tuesday morning make-out sessions were a rare occurrence and Daniel fully intended to make the most of it. From his enthusiastic response, it appeared Erik had the same idea, and Daniel found himself giggling against Erik's lips.

Panting, Erik broke away with a flashing smile.

"And I wasn't exactly sure what to do about a ring."

"Not sure of my ring size?" Daniel teased.

"Oh no. I know *exactly* how big your hands are." Erik's voice dropped low and husky. "But not in any way it's appropriate to explain to a jeweler."

Daniel's face flushed and a heat begin to simmer low in his belly. He shifted to adjust his pants, which suddenly seemed too snug. He looked up at Erik, who was blinking his long brown eyelashes slowly; his eyes were hazy and hot, and he was clearly aware exactly how badly Daniel wanted him.

"Plus, I *really* wasn't sure how to show her my frame of reference." Erik tried to keep a straight face.

Daniel's laugh burst out as Erik dissolved into hooting laughter. This was something different, something he shared only with Erik: the ability to laugh in bed. Or, on their way to bed, at least. Daniel wasn't about to quibble with the details.

So what if this wasn't the proposal he'd envisioned all those lonely years ago? So what if it hadn't gone as he'd dreamed? Here he was, with a man who was smart and kind and who wanted to marry *him*. Daniel loved him, and he loved Daniel. They laughed together. Who cared that they argued? They *laughed* together.

"Yes," he said definitively.

Erik quieted, his eyes still dancing. "Really?"

"Yes. Really. Even if you still haven't technically asked me."

"Daniel, will you marry me?"

Daniel lit up from the inside. This was really happening.

"Yes. Will you marry me?"

"Yes."

TWO DAYS LATER, DANIEL DIPPED a spoon in the sauce he was making, blew on it and tasted it. "Mmm, not enough salt. And maybe some more white wine."

"What else needs to be done?" Erik called as he charged through the front door.

"Vacuuming?" Daniel called back. "The table needs to be moved, and get the plates and stuff out there—"

Erik jogged into the kitchen, slung his arm around Daniel's waist as he stood at the stove and kissed Daniel's cheek. "I'm so sorry I'm late, babe. Dr. Selvig wouldn't shut up, and then I hit traffic on the 901 and—"

"Actually, I'm not that stressed. That's weird, right? It's not our engagement party; it's just family dinner. I promise I'll be stressed for the engagement." Daniel dipped the spoon in the sauce and held it to Erik's mouth. "Here, taste this."

Erik groaned. "Oh god, babe, that is awesome. Your cooking is getting better and better."

"Thanks." Daniel smiled sheepishly. "It's still not quite right, though."

"Maybe some more salt?" Erik headed back toward the living room.

"Exactly what I was thinking." Daniel nodded his head, grabbing the salt shaker. "Also, come here and give me another kiss."

"Anything you say, chef." Erik spun quickly around and headed back to him with a huge smile on his face. "I am yours to command."

"Dork," Daniel whispered before kissing him. "Don't ever change."

Erik chuckled low and deep in his throat and glanced down at his watch. "Oh, I know that look. And I don't think we have time for a quickie, love. I'm worried you're going to start freaking out in a couple of minutes."

"No, it's just family dinner. No freaking out." Daniel laughed as Erik stepped back.

"I'll run the vacuum and then we can both move the table, okay?"

"Once this gets in the oven, I can help with the plates and stuff." Daniel recklessly sloshed wine over the chicken in the Dutch oven. "It just needs to simmer a little longer, I think."

It was the first time they were combining their groups of friends, mixing several strong personalities, and Daniel was already freaking out inside. He took a long slug of wine from the bottle to calm his nerves. His work friends from Co-Op, they tended to be a bit, a bit flakey. Lord knew he loved them, but they were. And Erik's friend Annika was anything but. She was direct and blunt and honestly didn't have much of a sense of humor. Plus, she hated Daniel, or seemed to. Kate was Kate, and he already knew she hated Annika. And then Antonio was so quiet; who knew what he really thought?

Yeah, it was going to be an interesting evening.

ANNIKA ARRIVED WITH ANTONIO. As usual, she was dressed to the nines in very expensive clothes that Daniel was slightly in awe of. Erik had mentioned that she spent so much time digging in the dirt and liked to splurge on fancy clothes to wear when she wasn't working. Daniel thought it was more likely that it was easier to intimidate and feel superior to other people when she could look down on them from the heights of a Louboutin heel.

"Hello, darling," she said to Erik as she swept off her cape and handed it to Daniel without even looking at him.

Erik kissed both her cheeks. "Daniel and I are so glad you could make it, Annika."

"You know I wouldn't miss a chance to chat with you and Antonio outside of work," she cooed flirtatiously. Daniel spun on his heel and pretended to gag as he stalked away to hang up her cape.

"Who the fuck actually wears a cape?" he whispered to Kate a few minutes later in the kitchen, as they worked to put dinner on the plates. "Especially over to your friend's house for dinner?"

"People who are pretentious as fuck," Kate whispered back. "Or, you know, the Phantom of the Opera."

Daniel snorted.

"I mean, they're all over the style magazines these days," Kate continued. "But, yeah. Over to your friend's house for dinner, with that outfit on; she's clearly making a statement."

"Yes." Daniel carefully carved the roast chicken. "And that statement is, 'I can't believe the gutter trash you choose to spend your time with instead of sharing your life with me.'"

"You think she's jealous?"

"Oh god, yes." Daniel set slices of roast chicken on the plates Kate was holding out for him. "She wants Erik in the worst way and she's so fucking angry that she can't get him interested."

"I mean, he's gay." Kate raised her eyebrow. "Does she not get how that works?"

"Well, the last time we went out for drinks, she really pissed me off, and I might have offered to grab him and give her an explicit physical demonstration." Daniel wrinkled his nose as Kate burst out laughing. "Yeah, it was awkward after that. Vodka was involved. It was not my finest moment."

"That might explain why she's refused to even acknowledge your presence since she got here," Kate whispered. "Why did she even come here if she hates you so much?"

"Oh, she'd never give up the chance to hang out with Erik." Daniel glanced into the living room, where Annika was perched on the edge of an armchair with her legs crossed at the ankles and tucked under the chair and was swirling a glass of wine as she chatted with Erik and Antonio. "She always looks like she's posing for a magazine photospread."

"Is she just out there completely ignoring Carynne?" Kate glared at her.

"Probably. Erik will make sure Carynne's okay, though."

"Yeah." Kate drizzled sauce over the chicken. "You want some of the sauce on this couscous, too?"

"Yes, please." Daniel continued slicing. "I feel bad about the fact that I'm just glad that Stasia couldn't make it tonight."

Kate burst out in a raucous laugh. "Oh god, I'm not. I would pay good money to see that blood match."

Daniel laughed. "I know, right? Can you imagine?"

"Oh, Stasia would not be putting up with any of her shit. She'd be calling her out on everything."

"Exactly."

"Stasia would wipe the floor with Annika; what, are you kidding me with this?"

"It would be nice to see, I'll admit. But just not tonight." Daniel smiled enigmatically as he put the last of the chicken on the last plate.

"It's too bad Stefan couldn't be here." Kate sighed. "I could really use some weed."

"He offered to make some of his 'special brownies' for dessert." Daniel chuckled.

"Aw, why the fuck did you say no?"

"I didn't. He called this morning, said his dealer is having some supply troubles."

"God, I would have paid good money to see Fuckface Annika high as a kite."

"Fuckface Annika, that's what we're calling her now?"

"I'd call her Bitchface Annika, but I don't want to group her in with the very fine bitches that I am happy to be associated with."

"You honestly think she's going to eat a brownie?"

"No, you're right." Kate sneered as she looked out in the living room again. "She looks like she eats only steamed skinless chicken breast and the souls of the innocent."

Daniel laughed. "Have I told you you're my favorite?"

"Not today." Kate curtsied flippantly. "Why is Erik even friends with her?"

"Oh." Daniel shrugged one shoulder. "They've been friends for a long time; they've seen each other through some hard times, things like that. Erik being with me has definitely put a strain on their relationship. Erik's really not happy that she can't see past her own issues but he keeps hoping she will. I don't know. I don't really care at this point. I've accepted she's not my friend, and I'm not going to try to win her over any more."

"But, I still don't understand why Erik doesn't just say to her, 'Dude, this is the guy I'm in love with; either you warm up to him or you can fucking hit the road.'"

"He says she's working on it. She's really important to him, and they've known each other so long..." Daniel trailed off.

"Hey, everything going okay in here, you two?" Erik stood at the kitchen door. "What can I help with?"

"You can help get these plates ready to serve." Daniel replied. "For god's sake, wipe the edges, put some garnish on it, make it look fancy, you know."

"You don't have to try to impress her, love," Erik said quietly, kissing Daniel's cheek as he took the plates from him.

"I'm not trying to impress her. I'm trying not to give her a chance to complain."

"OKAY, SO WHAT'S UP, GUYS?" Kate set her now-empty dinner plate on the coffee table. They were all finishing their dinner, sprawled around the living room: Daniel and Erik on large cushions on the floor; Kate, Antonio and Carynne on the couch; Annika still perched in the armchair. "You guys never organize family dinner nights, so what's going on?"

Daniel glanced at Erik, who broke out in a huge grin and nodded. "We're getting married."

"What!" Kate shrieked as Carynne started clapping. "No fucking way!"

Antonio got up to shake their hands. "Congratulations."

Kate scampered up and dropped herself in Daniel's lap, grabbed his face and gave him a huge smacking kiss on the cheek. "Why didn't you tell me this was even a discussion you were having, you prick!"

Daniel laughed. "It was kind of a surprise, to me at least."

"I'd been thinking about it for a while," Erik explained. "It just seemed the right time."

"Weighing your options," Annika said darkly. She scowled as she pushed her chicken and couscous around her plate.

Carynne beamed. "I could tell something amazing had happened. You are both pulsating with such amazing energies."

"Tell us the story," Kate demanded. "All the gushy romantic details."

"Oh," Daniel began, catching Erik's eye and laughing. "Well, you know Erik. He was very professorial and hot. Very serious and earnest. And I was kind of clueless and excitable. There was a lot of kissing. You know how it goes."

"Details, Danny, I want details." Kate smacked him on the arm. "Not this bullshit glossing over things."

"No, I am being completely serious." Daniel giggled. "There was talk of tax benefits and investment properties and everything."

"Oh, Erik," Kate scolded as she glared at him. "You did not."

"I did." Erik shoved at Antonio, who'd started laughing loudly. "Daniel says he's the clueless one in this relationship, but I think maybe it's me." Erik laughed along so hard he could barely finish his sentence.

Everyone joined in with laughter, even Annika, who couldn't help but crack a smile. Watching their friends' faces as they all laughed and teased each other, Daniel was relieved. The engagement party would be a piece of cake.

SIX MONTHS BEFORE THE WEDDING

GOOD MORNING, DANIEL!

Congratulations on setting your date and reserving your venue! Good work! Your calendar entry is saved! Fourteen more items have been added to your checklist. (Select and purchase invitations. Select and purchase save-the-date cards. Honeymoon destinations and birth control contraindications list: 107 sub-checklist items. Click here for more.)

Click here to add or modify list entries. Showing 1-6 out of 70 checklist entries left to complete.

What's Trending on Aurora? Don't Abandon Your Paleo Diet Lifestyle on Your Wedding Day: See What's Hot In Caveman Wedding Apparel! Click here to read the article about your next wedding must-have!

Have a great day, Daniel!

Love,

Aurora

**

Click on checkboxes to mark task as complete, or on task name to edit/modify.
<u>*Unsubscribe*</u> *from reminders.*

"THE TOTAL NUMBER OF CHECKLIST entries never goes down," Daniel said, frowning at his phone. It's late on a Friday night in mid-November.

"What?" Erik looked up from his laptop. He was finishing his applications for summer dig grants.

"No matter how many things we check off Aurora's list, she always says there's seventy checklist entries left to complete."

"Again, it is an *it*, not a *she*. And it could be there's a glitch in the counter."

"It's just discouraging. It's like we're never going to get to the end of this checklist." Daniel sighed.

"Maybe we won't. Maybe this is all an alternate reality or a massive loop in the space-time continuum—"

"You think you're being funny, but you're not."

"Oh, Danny." Erik slung his arm around Daniel's shoulders. "You think I'm hilarious."

Daniel pretended to frown again, then grinned. "Yes. Most of the time, yes I do. And most of the time, you're even being hilarious on purpose."

Erik kissed him roughly on the lips and grinned back.

"At least that's one thing we can check off right away. We don't need no stinkin' birth control, and we don't have to worry about contraindications with our honeymoon destination." Daniel tapped gleefully at his phone. "Goodbye, stupid birth control checklist, and goodbye to your evil 107 sub-checklist items."

"What do we have to plan tonight?" Erik clapped his hands together and rubbed them briskly. They'd been cooperating recently, trying to divvy up the planning a bit more equally, and their team approach was apparent in their current state of relative bliss.

"Paper products. Invitations, save-the-date cards and possibly also the place-cards and ceremony programs, depending on the style, the theme and the cost."

"Excellent." Erik shoved his computer to the side. He rested his elbows on his knees, ready to dig in. "Do we have anything so far?"

"Well, I started requesting quotes and samples a while ago, so yes. We have a stack of things to sort through. I vote we start with the invitations, put them in three piles—yes, no and maybe—and then we rank everything in the 'yes' pile, and discuss everything in the 'maybe' pile."

"Sounds like as good a plan as any."

Daniel dumped small rectangular sample pieces of card stock out of three large manila envelopes onto the coffee table in front of them. Erik picked the first card up.

"Tacky," Daniel said immediately. "It looked much nicer on the website."

"Agreed," Erik set the card down. "Our first unanimous decision of the evening."

Daniel picked up the next card. "Now, I like this background color, and I like this font, but I'm not crazy about the weight of the paper or the color of the printing."

"We need to be taking notes on this," Erik grabbed his computer and swiftly opened a blank spreadsheet. He typed in Daniel's comments.

"What's your take on it?" Daniel handed the card to him.

"Yes, I think the paper feels cheap and flimsy." Erik held it close to his face to take a closer look. "And the ink is too thin."

"I don't know about the thinness of the ink, but it seems like it's just not as classy as some of the others."

"I vote we put it in the 'maybe' pile, with reservations. We'll revisit it, if we need to."

"An excellent idea, love." Daniel smiled.

Erik picked up the next sample card and carefully examined it. "Of course, we need to balance the quality with the cost, but this is just another cheap one. I vote 'No.'"

They worked quickly through the pile, with most of the options landing in the "no" pile, several in the "maybe" pile, and no cards in the "yes" pile.

"I think you're being too demanding," Daniel said. "These are just invitations, we can't go hog wild with them. We've got a lot of other things to pay for."

"But if we're already paying for them, we should at least get the best quality we can. Why spend a ridiculous amount of money on flimsy crap, when we could pay just a bit more and get some really nice stuff?"

"I suppose we're only getting married once—"

"Thank god," Erik interrupted fervently. He picked up another card, this one in the shape of a dog bone. "And this is...?"

"Oh god, don't even with this one. This is—this is one of the first samples I requested. I thought we needed a theme."

"You thought we needed a theme and you went with dog bones?" Erik grinned.

"Well, you know, I was going with one of your proposal non-ideas—"

"Non-idea? It was a perfectly valid proposal idea."

"I was desperate to get started checking things off the list. I thought we clearly needed a theme, so I thought wouldn't it be adorable to have, you know, dog things. It'd be cute. Everyone loves dogs."

"No." Erik shook his head. "No, we don't need a dog theme for our wedding. We don't even have a dog."

"No, admittedly, it wasn't one of my better ideas." Daniel plucked the card out of Erik's hand with a dismissive air. "It was one of those three a.m., wine-soaked Internet research nights when you were at your place."

"Clearly, I can't leave you alone at three a.m. anymore."

Daniel grinned and kissed him.

Erik sighed as he broke away. "But we definitely need to decide on ink color."

"A one-track mind." Daniel smiled ruefully. "Okay, yes, let's get this figured out."

"First, we definitely need to research the paper to find out what's the best, and the font needs to be..." Erik grabbed his computer and began feverishly typing away, mumbling to himself.

"So, we're done with all these?" At Erik's vague nod, Daniel began to tidy up all the samples, sliding them back in the giant envelopes. He stacked all the loose papers on the coffee table into a tidy pile.

Twenty minutes later, Erik was still staring at his computer, shaking his head and muttering. Daniel washed the dinner dishes.

An hour later, Daniel was tired and ready for bed.

"Erik?"

"Yeah, babe, I'll be there in a minute," Erik said. "I just want to finish looking up some things..."

"Oh, dear god, I've created a monster," Daniel muttered as he climbed into bed.

WHEN DANIEL WOKE UP, ERIK was slurping coffee at the breakfast table and muttering at his computer.

"What's your opinion on Bohemian stationery?"

"Huh?" Daniel could barely keep his eyes open as he poured his coffee.

"Cards from the Czech Republic. Stationery for the invitations."

"I know Sherlock thinks it's nice. That's about it."

"No, seriously." Erik glanced up at him over his laptop screen. "We want an invitation that feels nice in the hand, a nice heavy weight that feels formal and not cheap and ephemeral."

"Using the word 'ephemeral' before eight a.m.? So not cool," Daniel said under his breath as he poured in milk and sugar. "I am just not sure that the invitations warrant this much research," he said more loudly. "I mean, yes, we definitely need to decide on them, and I really, really appreciate your interest in them, but I think we can just go with the kind of standard—"

"Hey, you obsessed for almost an entire week over whether or not cream-colored table cloths would work with ecru napkins."

"True." Daniel slurped his coffee and sighed with satisfaction. "Okay, then I will have to state for the record that I have absolutely no opinion on stationery from the Czech Republic. I didn't know that was something to know about."

"Ah." Erik went back to frowning at his computer and typing quickly.

Daniel poured cereal and milk into a bowl and shuffled to the table.

"And I sent you an email with links to different fonts and ink colors. If you could rank them in your order of preference, we can get started narrowing them down."

"Oh god," Daniel said around a mouthful of cereal. "Okay. Yeah. I can do that."

Half an hour later, Daniel walked downstairs to Co-Op, said hello to Stasia and checked his phone. Seven emails, all from Erik, all asking for his "order of preference" on background color, paper weight, inks and fonts. He sighed and poured himself another cup of coffee. This was going to be a long day.

Two days later, Daniel arrived home to find Erik with his feet on the coffee table, holding two paper rectangles up in the air.

"Do you prefer linen? Or cotton?"

"Oh dear god. I'm so glad you're the one going bonkers over this one." Daniel dumped his bag on the floor and slumped on the couch next to Erik. He squinted at the paper. "Which one is which?"

"Linen," Erik said as he shook one card, then the other. "Cotton."

"From this distance, I can't really tell them apart. Is there a price difference?"

"A bit. I'm not actually sold on either one, I'm just trying to keep our options open."

"Well, we need to start narrowing down those options." Daniel's stomach rumbled loudly. "I'm going to go start dinner."

"Ok. I'm going to need the aesthetic design plans for the reception, so we can make sure the place card holders match."

"We are eating dinner first," Daniel declared. "I am not discussing aesthetic design plans with you on an empty stomach. That will only end in tears." He went into the kitchen and started pulling things out of the cupboard and fridge. Fajitas, he decided. Easy, quick, yummy and they had all the stuff to make them. Perfect. It was nice to plan something that was finite. Wedding planning was like a giant malicious octopus, where everything was nefariously interconnected and nothing could be decided without first deciding forty-seven other things. Fajitas, that was more his planning speed.

"Babe, what kind of vases will the table flowers be in?" Erik called.

"Uhh, regular ones? Just glass vases. The kind with the, uhh, the bulb kind of a thing at the bottom."

"Because this site here has these birch bark place-card holders on clearance, and I think they'd go really well with some of these mock-up invitations I've made."

"Birch bark?" Daniel swore under his breath as his knife slipped on a pepper and nearly sliced his thumb. "I mean, yeah. That could work."

"They've got matching birch bark vase holders that might be nice, too."

"I'm not sure what a birch bark vase holder would look like with the arrangements we've already decided on, babe." Daniel swiped everything into the hot frying pan.

"But we didn't order those arrangements yet. We could still change our minds." Erik came in and put the tortillas in the oven to warm.

"That's true."

"I just—looking at the photos on that site, it's really sparked something in my head, and I think we could make it really classic and personal and *us*."

Erik hadn't really taken the initiative on any of their planning so far, and Daniel wanted to be supportive of Erik's need to perfect the invitations and everything that went along with them.

"Okay, let's take a look at the photos and see what we can do." Daniel smiled.

Good morning, Daniel!

Congratulations on setting your date and reserving your venue! Good work! Your calendar entry is saved! Thirty-four more entries have been added to your checklist. (Register for gifts. Delegate Bachelorette/ Bachelor Party responsibilities. Finalize guest list. Click here for more.)

What's Trending on Aurora? Until Death Do Us Part— Or Not: This Summer's Hottest Zombie Themed Weddings! Click here to read the article about your next wedding Must-Have!

**

Click on checkboxes to mark task as complete, or on task name to edit/modify. Unsubscribe from reminders.

Daniel and Erik stood in the homewares section of the department store each holding a raygun-like apparatus.

"So, we just go around and bloop the price tags of anything we want to add to the register, and the computer arranges it all in a list that people can search." Daniel glanced around the store and tried to decide where to start.

Erik stared down at the machine in his hand. "Anything we want?"

"Yeah, anything. It all goes on the list, and then guests can come and look us up on the store's registry and buy things from it."

"I want a drill. Like, a nice, powerful drill."

"Then we'll head to the hardware section. Do you want to go there first, or should we do all these plates and dishes and pans first?"

"I don't want stupid china," Erik declared. "Those plates you only use at Christmas? I think that's a terrible idea."

"Oh, I agree. Let's go with nice plates we can use every day without freaking out of if one of them breaks."

They stare at the wall of plates in front of them, daunted by the sheer number of choices.

"And this doesn't even include all the ones in those catalogues on the shelf," Daniel whispered. "The salesperson said there are even more color choices in there."

"What have we gotten ourselves into?" Erik whispered back.

Twenty-five minutes later, they stood at the display table, arguing over their choices.

"That one is too floral. It's too much. It's distracting from the food."

"It'll look really nice before the food is served, though."

"Well, I don't like it." Erik sniffed.

"You haven't liked any of my choices so far," Daniel muttered.

"What about this one?"

"That's green."

"So?"

"We don't have anything in our house that would go with that shade of green."

"So?"

"So, every time we use the plates, it will be this giant horribly painful clash of colors. No, we're not doing that one."

"Well, then, what about this one?" Erik pointed to a different plate, simple and classic.

"Yes, I like that one."

Erik rubbed his chin. "I don't know. What about this pattern, but in a different color?"

"Oh, dear god." Daniel shook his head.

By the time the afternoon finally dragged to a close, they had had three arguments, two breaks for coffee and snacks, and one heated make-out session behind a large display while choosing their bedding choices.

They both agreed that luxurious sheets, the kind so comfortable you never ever want to get out of bed, were exactly what they wanted. They registered for six sets, in varying price ranges, and a down comforter they hoped several people would chip in for because it was eye-crossingly expensive.

"I want our bed to be an oasis." Daniel stretched out on the display bed, knocking several throw pillows to the floor.

"Oh, do you?" Erik tossed the pillows onto a nearby display, then lay down next to him on his back, crossing his ankles and folding his hands across his stomach.

"It needs to be our little—our escape. Our refuge. We don't have to be anyone but ourselves there. Just you and me."

DANIEL'S WORK ON THE WINDOWS for the Reinholt house quickly became a stress he could have lived without. When Daniel visited the worksite one day, he found they'd installed some windows in different orientations than he'd designated and had altered the sequence of another set. The foreman changed the delivery dates twice and gave him inconsistent measurements for the final size needed. Daniel wanted to pull out his hair.

Daniel chomped on a pencil as he laid out an intricate design of colored glass pieces for one of the windows in his studio behind Co-Op. He squinted at it, then stepped away to view it from a distance. He rearranged several pieces, all shades of blue, and stepped back again to see how it looked.

Erik popped his head through the doorway. "Hey, I'm back. The groceries are upstairs. I put away the milk and meat, but Dr. Nillson just called and told me he's scheduled an emergency midterm prep help session for the students and I have to be there."

"We're supposed to finalize the menu tonight," Daniel reminded him.

"I know, but it's midterms, and a bunch of these kids are really panicked and needing some extra help—"

"The menu *has* to be finalized tonight." Daniel could feel his stomach acid beginning to burn.

"I'm sorry, Danny. This is my job. He'll have my balls if I don't go. Just decide on the menu, and everything will be great; I know it." Erik gave him a quick kiss on the cheek and left in a hurry.

Daniel wanted to shout after him, wanted to scream, in fact. So far, it seemed to him as if Daniel and Daniel alone was making most of the nitty-gritty wedding decisions, and he was sick and tired of it. Daniel's mind raced with questions. Why was Erik being such an asshole? Was he really so anti-traditional wedding? Did he really not care about giving themselves and their guests a wedding to remember? Did he have cold feet? Did he not want to get married at all? Was he regretting proposing after all? Had he decided he didn't really want to spend the rest of his life with Daniel? Did Daniel really want to spend the rest of his life with such an asshole?

They had not found a comfortable compromise, arguing over Erik's seeming lack of care for, and Daniel's seeming obsession with, the details of the wedding. Daniel was angry the planning was never Erik's priority;

Erik was angry Daniel put it before everything else. Daniel had to believe that it was going to get better, that they would start getting along again once the wedding was over. This stress wasn't indicative of what the rest of their lives together would be, right? Surely it would get better.

Daniel thought about mentioning to Erik that he should spend tonight at his own apartment. Just one night without gritting his teeth; one night to sprawl across his bed without worrying about keeping to his own side; one night without the anger-tinged dance of trying to coexist when they weren't getting along.

Telling him directly seemed too abrupt and scary. It might open a can of worms, a pit of darkness that Daniel didn't want to go anywhere near.

His stomach rumbled. He'd been so engrossed in working on the windows he'd skipped lunch, and it must be close to dinnertime. He'd have to go get something to eat, or his hands would be too shaky for the delicate process of placing and soldering. He sighed and turned off his soldering iron.

As he walked through Co-Op in the near-dark, he heard the pounding of someone running down the stairs from his apartment. He nearly collided with Erik coming in the door.

"Oh." Erik stopped abruptly. "You're stopping?"

"I need dinner. Why are you still here? Did you eat?"

"They're ordering pizza for the study session. I'll eat there." Erik shoved a dark shape at Daniel, his ventilator mask. "I saw you're about to start soldering, so I just replaced the filters in here. Don't forget to turn on your exhaust fan."

Daniel was surprised, and felt bad for all the swearing he'd been doing in his head. Maybe Erik wasn't just going to skip out on their life together.

"I got you some of those microwave burritos you love, even though they are completely awful for your health. They're quick, and I know you want to get back to work as soon as you can. And broccoli was on sale, and if you start it boiling while the burrito cooks, it should be ready by the time the microwave's done, and then you can at least have some vegetables with your death burrito," Erik said in a rush.

"Thanks." Daniel sighed.

"I don't know when I'll be back tonight. I love you."

Daniel nodded. "Love you, too."

"And don't forget your exhaust fan." Erik spun on his heel and pushed the building's front door open.

"How's it going, baby?" Erik said brightly as he walked through the door of Daniel's apartment two weeks later. "What are you up to?"

"Ugh." Daniel groaned. He gestured at the stacks of papers around him on the table. "Orders for Co-Op, because I'm apparently the only person who has a calculator. Trying to write my vows, trying not to dream up murder scenarios for the foreman at the Reinholt job. Right now I'm trying to think up songs for the reception. I'm torn because I want 'YMCA,' but I don't want the YMCA—"

"I vote yes on the 'YMCA.' I love that song."

"My mother loves that song. She thinks dancing to it proves to everyone how 'okay' she is with 'the gays.'"

"Please don't ever tell her what the song is really about." Erik laughed.

"Oh god, no. No, no, no." Daniel said. "Other than that stuff, I have some sketches I need to finish for the windows because things aren't working out quite how I wanted them with the lighting. Apparently the landscaping has changed, and they're taking down more trees, so there's more light and it's kind of developing into a headache."

"Umm." Erik took a deep breath. "So, other than that, your stress level is good?"

"I wouldn't say it's good, but it's—wait, what is going on?" Daniel looked up, narrowing his eyes.

"Just—before I tell you this, I want you to remember that in the big scheme of things, in the big picture of the rest of our lives, this one little thing is only a blip—"

"Oh, my god." Breathing heavily through his nose, Daniel placed both hands flat on the table in front of him. "What's wrong? Who's dying?"

"No one. No one is dying." Erik rushed to put his hand on Daniel's shoulder as he sat down in the chair next to him. "It's important for you to remember that."

"Spit it out, Erik," Daniel gritted out.

"You're going to hyperventilate."

"Then I guess you should just tell me, now shouldn't you?"

"Okay, umm. I got a call today during my office hours. The, uhh, the museum has been shut down by the EPA—"

"What?" Daniel shrieked. "For how long?"

Erik smiled weakly. "They are not willing or able to give an expected time of reopening, as of right now."

"You're fucking kidding me."

"No. No, I'm not. They've found asbestos in one of the older wings yesterday afternoon and have to go through a whole abatement thing, and it's just a giant mess—"

"But we can still have our reception there, right?"

Erik took another deep breath. "No. The whole thing has to be sealed off."

"Oh, my fucking god." Daniel put both hands in his hair and pulled slightly. This wasn't happening. This just wasn't happening. "What are we going to do?"

"Well, they're really, really sorry, and they've already scouted out some other locations on campus where we could have it. They're going to refund all the money we paid them, even the deposit, and get us a deal on using another space."

"Oh, my fucking god," Daniel repeated.

"So, the gymnasium is available—"

"They want us to get married on a basketball court?"

"Yeah, I'm not in favor of that, either." Erik shook his head. "Or the hockey arena, either."

"Oh, my god."

"But!" Erik smiled an over-bright and enthusiastic smile. "The art museum is available."

"That place will hold, like, seven people." Daniel shook his head in disbelief. "It's not even a museum, it's like a tiny shed on campus. There's no room for anything there, no tables, no dance floor, no nothing."

"We could get a tent. We could do the ceremony in the art museum, and have the tent in the gardens outside, and it will be beautiful, baby."

Daniel paused to take calming breaths through his nose. "That might work. If we do that, we need to look into tent rental, and tables—"

"And a portable kitchen, or something—"

"Oh fucking hell, there's no kitchen there for the caterer to work in. Or one anywhere nearby." Daniel dropped his forehead to the table with a thunk. "The whole menu was planned with her having an on-site kitchen. The entire menu will have to change. Do you think the museum restaurant can handle the cooking, or do we need to find a new caterer?"

"The woman I spoke with didn't think it was possible; the kitchen has been contaminated, as well. But it's okay, baby, we can do it."

"Finding a caterer at such short notice…" Daniel picked his head up and began rubbing firmly at his temples. "And a portable bar—"

"I'm sure the tent rental company will know about all of that." Erik rubbed Daniel's back.

"And the place settings. And probably the table design. And definitely the seating charts."

"Maybe, maybe not." Erik waggled his head, considering, then bit his lip.

"Maybe we could do a buffet, right?" Daniel swept both hands through his hair. "A dessert buffet, or a sausage buffet, or something that doesn't involve a lot of wait staff or something like that, right?"

"Also..." Erik began.

Daniel grabbed a blank piece of paper and a pen, furiously scribbling down notes. "Also, what?"

"They asked me to go do the pre-dig conference, to fly over there and schmooze with donors, handle the last-minute site details and show the big shots around while we do enough digging to give them the flavor of the project."

"That's a really big deal." Daniel smiled weakly. "Isn't it?"

"Yeah." Erik smiled shyly. "It's a really big deal. I mean, it's because Dr. Nikerson had appendicitis and is in the hospital and can't go. But it would mean a lot of great opportunities to meet some important people and really get my name out there. But, it's in two weeks."

"For how long?"

"Ten days."

Daniel glanced at his calendar, full of appointments and things crossed out and overwritten, their wedding date encircled with a giant heart in red marker. "You'll get back three days before the wedding?"

"Yeah." Erik shook his head. "I feel like I really should say 'no.' I don't want to leave you here to deal with this—"

"This is a huge deal for you, and for your career." Daniel wrinkled his nose and tried to smile brightly. "You have to go."

"We should talk about it some more later." Erik began rummaging in the fridge. "Right now, I'm making dinner."

"I mean, you'll still have email access, right? We can do a lot of work via email, right?"

"I'll have Internet access when I'm in Stockholm, but out at the site, probably not."

"No Internet?"

"Maybe not even cellphone. It was pretty chancy coverage when I was there the last time."

"Oh god." Daniel rubbed both his temples with his fingertips. Could they really re-plan their entire wedding in so short a time? "Well, we can try to make it work."

Erik set a pan on the stove and turned it on. "We'll talk about it over dinner. It's too big a decision to make on the fly."

"Mm-hmm." Daniel pecked at his tablet. "I wonder if Aurora still has those caterers' brochures and menus stored, or even just their contact information."

The only sound from the kitchen was the hiss of onions sautéing.

"A-ha!" Daniel crowed triumphantly. "She does!"

"*It* is not a *she. It* is a computer program that—"

"That is going to save our asses because she has everything stored in the cloud and even though I deleted all that caterer stuff off my phone, it's all still available," Daniel said happily. "She even has my notes still."

"*It*," Erik repeated wearily.

AFTER HIS MORNING SPENT CALLING around to caterers to check their availability, Daniel regretted pushing Erik to go to the conference. He sighed heavily as he hung up his phone after the fourth company told him there was no possible way they could accommodate another wedding that weekend.

"It's not even like we can change the date, at this point." Daniel blew out his breath. "The invitations are already sent out. I mean, thank god we weren't doing the 'choose your entrée' cards with the RSVPs."

"I think we had enough ridiculous pieces of cardboard in those envelopes," Erik said as he searched in his messenger bag for a particular file folder.

"Ridiculous pieces of cardboard that *you* picked out, love," Daniel reminded him.

"Mm-hmm."

"Erik, are you listening to me?"

"Danny, I have got to get this stuff done," he said impatiently. "I have to leave for class soon."

"Oh, no, sir. We have got to get *this* stuff done. This. Our wedding. The thing we are thousands of dollars in debt for. We're going to have one hundred guests arriving in three weeks, and we have absolutely nothing to feed them, or anything for them to do—"

"Except witness our marriage," Erik snapped. "The one thing that they really should be there for."

"Don't start this again."

"Start what again?"

"Your usual 'everything about this wedding is ridiculous and unnecessary' spiel. I've heard it enough."

"There is very little about this wedding that *doesn't* seem ridiculous or unnecessary."

"So your whole bit about how you wanted me to have the wedding of my dreams was just complete bullshit?"

"If I'd seen any part of this wedding that you were overjoyed or excited about, I'd be behind it one hundred percent. As it is, all I get is you bitching about having to make a choice from options you don't even really like."

"You know, sometimes, you are such an asshole," Daniel said, angrily, slamming his notepad down.

"Yeah, well, right back at you, babe." Erik stood up abruptly, slinging his bag over his shoulder.

"Where are you going? We're not done here—"

"I'm going to be late for class. We can finish this discussion tonight. I've got two classes this afternoon, so I won't be home before six or so." Erik's voice was tight with anger.

"Excellent. Then during your break between classes, you can call the tent rental people and figure out that situation." Daniel sneered. "I'm taking care of the caterers and the flowers and the rest of the ceremony. The *least* you could do is help out."

Erik made a savage noise in the back of his throat. "Fine."

"Fine."

"I love you." Erik said quietly as he paused by the door.

Daniel hesitated. His head was pounding. He wanted to vent his anger, his frustrations, just let out all the strain. Every time they had a disagreement, the stresses piled up. He couldn't let anything go; each annoyance, each snarl, each argument just made the next one feel ever more momentous and paralyzing. He felt spiteful and awful; he wanted to punch a wall, or smash a plate, or something, anything. It would be so satisfying right now to say something nasty and hurtful, especially to Erik, with his smug calm and *fucking asshole* face.

But he couldn't. That wouldn't be right. He loved Erik, even if he did want to slam a frying pan into his forehead sometimes.

"I love you, too," he said.

WHEN ERIK GOT HOME, HE did, in fact, have the tent rental figured out. The vendor would handle the tents, all the tables and chairs, even the dance floor.

"And the guy I talked to says he knows someone who's got connections at the culinary school, and they might be able to do the catering and cover the serving and all that."

"Good," Daniel said tightly, as he stood in the kitchen. "That's good. Thanks."

"Hey." Erik walked slowly up behind him. "I know—I know I can be an ass sometimes. We're just so wrapped up in this planning, it's driving me crazy."

"Yeah, I know." Daniel leaned stiffly against the counter. "It's driving me crazy, too."

"I know. I'm worried about you, Danny. You're not sleeping, you're barely eating."

"It's only a few more weeks." Daniel uncrossed his arms, trying to relax.

"Let's just—let's take tonight off, okay? I'm sorry I blew up at you, I'm sorry I'm leaving, I'm sorry this is all so stressful."

"There's so much—I have so much stuff to figure out, and more RSVPs to add and the seating chart—"

"Danny, please." Erik cautiously put his hands on Daniel's shoulders, as if he was waiting to see if Daniel would blow up.

"I…" Daniel faltered.

Erik dug his thumbs into Daniel's shoulder muscles, and Daniel groaned. He hadn't realized how tense his shoulders had gotten until Erik's massage sent tingles down to his fingertips.

"Come on, love," Erik whispered. "Just tonight. Let's just have a night for us."

Erik's hands slid lower, right to the knots between Daniel's shoulder blades, loosening them. Daniel rolled into his touch. Daniel couldn't remember the last time they'd made love. With a moan he dropped his head to his chest as Erik pressed harder.

"You know I love you, right?" Daniel asked, shakily. "I know I'm a raging bitch sometimes, and sometimes I just get so angry but I do—I love you."

The problems they had weren't even close to being fixed, but at least, for the moment, they weren't making a gaping fiery hole in Daniel's chest. His stomach churn slowed. Under Erik's hands, his body loosened, drawn toward Erik. Erik pressed his lips to the side of Daniel's neck and nuzzled at his ear.

Desire, want, lust burned low and hot in Daniel. His skin prickled; his nerves pinged; his senses heightened. He turned without a word and, taking Erik's hand, tugged him toward the bedroom.

"So, here's the RSVP section of the database." Daniel sighed as he turned his computer screen to show Erik. He clicked through the various fields in the database Aurora provided. "And when they send their little RSVP card back, we click here and it'll open up a new tab where we can add additional comments, like food allergies and seating preference and—"

"Seating preference?"

"Well, I think that's for where *we'd* like them seated. 'Let's not put Uncle Timothy right next to the bar' and that kind of thing."

"Ah. Okay." Erik grinned and then headed toward the bathroom. He emerged with his packed bag of toiletries.

"And part of me is thinking we'll just print out the addresses for the thank-you cards." Daniel grabbed a large stack of mail from the shelf. He dropped it with an impressive thud onto the kitchen table. "All these RSVP cards coming back are making my hands hurt just looking at them."

"Why didn't we do that for the invitations, again?"

"Because it's tacky. It's awful. It looks cheap."

"I just want to point out that three weeks ago, you asked me if it was possible to die from carpal tunnel syndrome."

"It was a low point, yes." Daniel cracked his knuckles as he sat on the creaking kitchen chair. "But I got over it. Those invitations needed to be addressed, and you've got horrific penmanship. So, there was only me."

Erik snorted.

"I feel guilty about not dropping you off at the airport tomorrow." Daniel opened the address spreadsheet and groaned as it took forever to load.

"No, you're already so stressed out; it'll just be even more stress to come with me." Erik set the open suitcase down on the bed and began to pack his things.

"Oh, no, it'll all work out just fine." Daniel pitched his voice higher, imitating his mother, then dropped it back to normal. "I've got to give the okay to the florist on swapping out the freesia, double-check with the caterers about possible allergens in everything, figure out place settings and start putting together my list of songs we absolutely have to have the DJ play. You need to start your list while you're away, ok?"

"Mm-hmm," Erik murmured as he struggled to get his travel adapter to fit back in its carrying pouch.

"Babe, did you hear me?"

"Uh-huh." He was still struggling with the pouch.

"Babe! Did you hear me?"

"Daniel! Yes, I did," Erik snapped. "I'm trying to get this thing in the fucking pouch, I need to not forget to bring my second hard drive, I need the files that Dr. Nillson forgot last time and I will not forget to put together a list of songs that I probably won't remember hearing on our wedding day."

"Look, I'm just trying to make it memorable." Daniel breathed sharply out of his nose in an attempt to stay calm. Blood pounded in his head. The biting edge of anger in Erik's voice was like a spark to a powder keg. Daniel's temper flared whenever Erik got testy.

"It will be memorable, Danny."

"I just want it to be—"

"Perfect. I know, Danny. I've been hearing that for months now." Erik tossed his travel adapter and a stack of file folders toward his suitcase. "But life still goes on, beyond wedding planning. I can't just drop everything to come up with a list of songs."

"What's that supposed to mean?"

"I mean, I've got this conference to go to, this one means *everything*. So much networking, and talking to people, and if I can't get the right people interested, my project is going nowhere. I'll have to start from the beginning."

"Look, I've got stuff going on too, aside from the wedding. You're not the only one who's stressed out, here."

"I know, I just—" Erik sighed.

"You just what?" Daniel put down his pen.

"To be honest, this wedding obsession of yours is really—I don't understand it."

"What do you mean? I'm so obsessed with this wedding because you are so *not* obsessed with this wedding, and so I have to make every decision by myself and keep track of every single thing so nothing gets missed and I—"

"You really don't have to do that."

"Yes, I do." Daniel snapped.

"No, you don't. Who's going to care if the napkins are cotton or linen or gingham or whatever—"

"*I'm* going to care."

"But I don't understand *why*, Danny. Why does it matter so much?"

"Because this is how weddings go! This is how they are done!" Daniel shouted. "Everyone knows how awful wedding planning is. It's used in every rom-com movie, and everyone knows how awful it is."

"Danny, that's ridiculous.

"It is *not* ridiculous!"

"Why do we have to do these things? Why can't we just go get married at City Hall, by ourselves? Why does it have to be in front of all these people, with all these hoops to jump through? What are you trying to prove?"

"I am not trying to prove anything!"

"I think you are. I think you're trying to prove to your family, and to the rest of the world, that we're normal, whatever that means. That we're just as good as them. That we're just like them, not in any way different, nothing to be afraid of."

"That's ridiculous."

"You're trying to fit us into the little box of what they're comfortable with—"

"I am not!"

"You are. Your family accepts that you're gay, but only if you're gay 'in the right way.'"

"What the hell is that supposed to mean?"

"So long as you get married and have kids and buy a house in the suburbs two miles away from the rest of them. They're fine with that."

"That's totally fucking ridiculous."

"Danny, I've met them. They don't like people who are different; they don't know how to accept 'different.'"

"Are you trying to tell me my family doesn't accept me?"

"No, Danny, they don't. You know they don't, and you've spent so much of your life trying to make that okay." Erik rearranged the clothes in his suitcase. "And I don't understand why you're trying so hard to win their approval."

"I am not trying to win their approval."

"Danny."

"I am not trying to win their approval."

"You wouldn't be so obsessed with all these little details if you weren't. You wouldn't be so organized, if you weren't."

"So, now I'm disorganized?"

"Danny, please." Erik looked up, his eyebrow raised. "We both know you're disorganized."

"I'm just—I'm so sick of being blamed for everything, and being told I'm all these awful things—"

"Since when is being disorganized an awful thing?"

"Since you *hate* disorganized people!"

"Danny, I don't hate you. I love you. You just drive me insane sometimes."

"All the time, lately. You haven't had a nice thing to say to me for weeks."

"You've had your head stuck in those wedding magazine for weeks. I haven't had a chance to say anything to you because you're too busy with the fucking table linens."

"You keep bringing up the linens as if they prove something, which is just fucking ridiculous. The linens is a new problem. With the buffet, we need different napkin options, and I have to figure out the next best option, without having to reorder the flowers, and the name cards, and everything we've already picked out, all over again."

"It's all ridiculous." Erik thumped his shoes into his suitcase. "It doesn't matter, and you're acting like it's going to cure cancer or something."

"You are so fucking infuriating sometimes."

"So are you." Erik looked as though he was grinding his teeth as he folded his clothes.

A cold, calm moment of clarity washed over Daniel. "You know what? I can't do this anymore."

"Do what, anymore?" Erik asked.

"This," he gestured at the table, piled high with wedding notes and paperwork. His sketches were smudged, everything had rings from coffee mugs on it; he couldn't find anything . "This wedding. This—everything."

Erik looked up from his packing.

"I can't take this stress. I can't—I can't function. I can't breathe anymore."

Erik dropped his half-folded shirt into his suitcase and watched Daniel.

"It's supposed to be easier than this, isn't it? This isn't supposed to be so hard. This can't be what the rest of our life is supposed to be like."

"Like what?"

"Like, we argue all the time, about every little thing. I can't remember the last time we agreed on *anything.*"

"Yesterday, we agreed on the favors we're giving out to everybody."

"That wasn't agreeing. That was you being frustrated and just giving up."

"I agreed."

"You gave up," Daniel insisted.

"What does that—why—?"

Daniel interrupted. "We need to agree; we need to compromise, which means we need to each take an interest."

"You take enough interest for the both of us, Danny."

"What the hell is that supposed to mean?"

"You're obsessed. You have not been able to spend one waking hour without talking about the wedding, needing to decide something about the wedding—"

"I just want it to be perfect!"

"It would be perfect for me if the man I fell in love with was standing next to me—"

"And I'm not the man you fell in with anymore?"

"You're—"

"You know what?" Daniel threw his pen down on his table. "Let's just call this what it is."

"And what is it?"

"A mistake. This is a mistake. You and I—getting married is a mistake."

"Danny, stop and think about what you're saying," Erik pleaded.

"Let's not—these things always drag on and on. Let's just tell it like it is and agree that we are ending this."

"Danny, that's not what I want." Erik sat down hard on the chair in the corner of their room.

"I'm sorry that's not what you want, Erik. That's what *I* want. This is just a ridiculous way to live."

"What's ridiculous about it? I love you and I thought you loved me—"

"I don't know that. I don't—this isn't what love should feel like. This doesn't feel like love." Daniel's throat tightened, and he was afraid he might start to cry.

Erik stared down at his hand and said nothing.

"It shouldn't be this hard, Erik. We shouldn't have to force ourselves to be civil to each other. We shouldn't be arguing about everything. We shouldn't be annoyed the minute we wake up."

"I'm not annoyed the minute we wake up—"

"You are, too. Don't—let's just give up, okay? We had a good run, we did our best, but it's just bashing our heads against the wall trying to move any further forward."

"Danny—"

"I'm—I'm done, Erik. I'm just done. I don't have anything left. I don't have anything left to give. I don't have any patience, I don't have any—anything. I've exhausted all my resources. I'm just—this is over, Erik."

"I don't think that. I don't want that."

"I've been waiting for this to happen. I've known this was coming for a long time," Daniel continued.

"Please, let's talk this over."

"This *is* over. I'm over this. I'm done."

"You don't love me anymore?"

"I don't know." Daniel took a deep breath and looked directly at Erik, in time to see something in his eyes shatter. "I'd like to think that I do, but I just don't know. And that's why I know this is over."

Erik sighed. "I'm not going to try to force you to stay together. This only works if we both want to be here."

"I know." Now that the difficult words were out, the words that had been bubbling under the surface of Daniel's skin for weeks and weeks, he felt at peace. "I'll go to Kate's to stay for a while."

"You've got a plan, already?"

"I've known this was coming, Erik. I could see that it was happening." Erik frowned at his hands.

"You could have said something," he said quietly.

"I'm saying something *now*. We've been so—I've been busy and you've been busy and we've just—we're lost. We've been scraping things together for months, trying to stick it out. We've been ignoring the fact that there's just nothing left here to be scraped together and just, please, Erik, let's let it go."

"I don't want—I—" Erik sighed, and sat heavily on the bed next to his suitcase. "Is this really what you want?"

Daniel nodded, keeping his lips pressed together. "My mind's made up." He didn't think he could say much more without bursting into tears.

"If you want, I will go stay at my place tonight," Erik said quietly. "Otherwise, I'm just going to keep pushing you to talk about it before you're ready, and that's not going to help anything. Maybe we could talk some more over lunch tomorrow."

"Yes, I think you should go. But I am done talking about it." Daniel swallowed hard. "Let's not drag this out and make this awful."

"This isn't already awful?" Erik laughed bitterly. "I'm pretty sure this qualifies as 'awful,' Danny."

"Just—you should go on your trip and go on the dig, and once you're busy, you will see how much better you feel. You will see that this is the right decision."

"Then you don't fucking know me at all, if you think I could think this was the right decision." Erik scrubbed at his eyes.

"That's exactly my point. We're just too different to be happy together."

"That statement doesn't make any sense to me." Erik stood up.

"You know it's true."

"I know—" Erik began angrily, then shook his head. "What I know doesn't matter any more. If you don't want to be together, then that's that. I can't make you want to be with me."

Daniel bit his lip, dropping his head to hide the tears in his eyes. He didn't know what to say.

"I guess it's a good thing I'm already packed," Erik said bitterly as he slammed his suitcase shut. "I'll get out of your hair."

Daniel sat, frozen, not knowing what to do, what else to say. He didn't want Erik to leave angry, but he couldn't deny he wanted Erik to leave.

"Goodbye, Daniel." Erik slammed the door shut behind him.

▯

A WEEK LATER, DANIEL SLOUCHED on the couch, watching TV. His eyes kept flickering back to Erik's canvas field jacket where it hung on the rickety coatrack near the door. He took another swig of his beer, trying to decide what to do.

It wasn't that it was Erik's "lucky jacket," or anything like that. It was just Erik's habit to wear it for every single dig. It had huge pockets for storing maps and tools and brushes and whatever else he didn't have enough hands for. Daniel knew Erik didn't take the time to leave the site to eat lunch, so he often kept snacks tucked away in the interior pocket.

Daniel sighed. He had a nagging worry, tiny and small in the back of his head: Erik would feel off-kilter at the dig without his jacket, off-balance and bothered by any replacement. The pockets wouldn't be in the right spot, or wouldn't be big enough. He'd be too warm in it, or too chilly. The collar would make his neck itch.

He sighed again. This break-up was going well, so far. He was still firmly in Stage One, the Ice Queen stage, where everything was crystal clear and nothing hurt too badly. He'd been through enough breakups to be able to see it for what it was, just a stage in the process of breaking up. But, this time, he didn't see any reason why Stage One couldn't just continue indefinitely. He could be calm and cool and collected. He could get his life in order. He could move on—all in Stage One—and never hurt about it all.

Yet, it bothered him that Erik would be leaving for his big dig, and he didn't have his coat. Erik was a man of routine, of order and habit. It would distress him, Daniel thought, to be deprived of those routines and habits. And because their break-up had gone far better than Daniel had thought it could possibly go, he saw no reason to be vicious or petty. He didn't want to knowingly increase Erik's discomfort. He really wished Erik well, the best of everything. Erik definitely deserved to be happy.

Daniel had burned several of his ex-boyfriend Matthew's things that he'd found in his apartment after their breakup: old notes and photos of them, even a hideous teddy bear Matthew had won at the state fair. It was a definite turning point in Daniel's life: standing in front of that burning pile of memories, feeling the beginning of the release of Matthew's hold over him.

But Daniel didn't want to do that to Erik's memory. Their breakup was nothing like his breakup with Matthew. It wouldn't be right or decent to burn Erik's things.

Daniel took another drink of his beer. He crossed and uncrossed his ankles where they were propped on the battered coffee table. His heart fluttered as he tried to figure out how he'd get the jacket, and the rest of his things, back to Erik. What would Erik do if Daniel just showed up on his doorstep with a box? Once it was clear he was just there on a cordial return-of-possessions errand, Erik would probably relax. Maybe they'd have a beer together, talk about how things had been for them apart.

Daniel played out in his head that scene, those possible conversations, polite and amicable. They all ended in one of them blurting out their dismay at their separation, vowing eternal love.

Clearly, Daniel was not going to deliver the jacket in person.

He could call him, ask Erik how he'd like to get the jacket back. Perhaps he'd suggest leaving it with Antonio, or another intermediary. That would be kind, yet efficient.

He put down the beer, wiped his mouth and picked up his phone with cold hands. He dialed Erik's cell number.

"We're sorry, but the number you have reached is out of service," the canned voice on the other end of the line whined in his ear.

Daniel frowned. Erik was supposed to be back from his conference, but maybe the dates had changed. Maybe he was still in Sweden, where his cell wouldn't work properly.

He sat up, planted his feet on the floor and dialed the number to Erik's apartment, just in case. After several rings, someone picked up.

"Hello?" It clearly wasn't Erik.

"Uhh... Antonio?" Daniel couldn't think of anyone else who might be answering Erik's phone.

"Yeah." Antonio sounded out of breath.

"Hey, this is Daniel. Is Erik there?"

"Danny, umm." Antonio paused. "Erik isn't here."

"Oh, well, no worries, then," Daniel said, brightly. "I'll just call him later."

"No, he's—he won't be here later, either. He's gone."

"What do you mean he's gone? He's supposed to be back from the conference." The fluttering in his chest dropped into a hollow feeling in his stomach.

"Yeah." Antonio paused. "Look, he got a big offer from the school there in Sweden. He's staying on there. He's not coming back after the dig."

"He's already gone and he's not coming back." Daniel's smile was hurting his face. "Okay then, well, thanks for answering the phone, I was just—"

"Look, I'm really sorry, Danny," Antonio broke in. "I didn't think it was my place to say anything. I wanted to, but—"

"No, don't worry about it." Daniel couldn't stop smiling as he pressed the phone to his ear. "It's fine."

"Danny, listen—"

"I have to go, Antonio. Thanks for letting me know. See you around." Daniel ended the call and tossed his cell on the coffee table. He bit his bottom lip, grabbed his bottle of beer and finished it off. He dropped his feet back on the coffee table with a heavy clunk and resolutely ignored the jacket on the coatrack, the sweater he knew was still in the closet, the pile of books on the side table—all things he'd have to figure out what to do with. He kept his eyes on the television and practiced breathing slowly and calmly.

Stage One was not over yet, not if Daniel had anything to say about it.

Day of Wedding

Congratulations on your big day, Daniel!

Don't forget to eat sensibly throughout the day and drink plenty of water! Dehydration and low blood sugar wreak havoc on weddings!

Take a deep breath and be sure to take a good look around you. Wedding memories are some of the most precious memories of your life!

And don't forget to tell your partner how happy you are to be marrying them!

All the best in your new life,
Aurora

P.S. Please take a moment to rate our app in the app store!

**

Check out Aurora's sister apps!

Eos can help organize your family planning needs, track basal temperatures and ovulation, as well as keeping track of potential baby names and registry items! Arinna can help you with financial organization, house-buying and mortgage calculation, as well as estate planning.

With the Aurora family of organizational apps, you and your new life partner can have it all!

DANIEL SPENT THEIR NOT-WEDDING DAY doing punishing menial labor alone in his apartment.

He re-caulked the shower and cleaned out the drains. He hand-washed all his wool sweaters and scarves and hats. He vacuumed all the furniture.

When the apartment was filled with a damp miasma and every available flat surface was covered with drying wool, he sat on the kitchen floor with a toothbrush and scrubbed the grout, until his fingers would no longer uncurl from around the handle.

🗌

Are you sure you want to uninstall Aurora? If you do, you will lose all your stored data, and will not be able to undo.

Daniel took a deep breath and clicked "yes." A small screen popped up: *Deleting all Aurora files. Please wait.* Daniel stared at his phone, transfixed by the small wheel spinning on his screen.

Uninstall complete.

A surge of regret and a rising panic rushed over him because he knew he could never get those things back. All the data from months of planning wasn't coming back. *Erik* wasn't coming back. Nothing would ever be the same again. He was suddenly nauseated and cold, as if he had the flu. He looked at his phone one last time and burst into tears.

He'd heard from Erik only once since he'd walked out, just an email letting Daniel know he'd contacted all the wedding vendors to cancel and to discuss whatever refunds they could get; it wasn't much. He detailed how he thought it best to begin paying off the remaining wedding-that-didn't-happen debt. Daniel had agreed, numbly. It was more than fair and reasonable that they split the costs fifty-fifty, but then, of course, Erik could be the most fair and reasonable person on the planet. He'd said he'd been offered a position at the university in Stockholm and he was going to take it. He wouldn't be back to Tallenburg until mid-winter.

Daniel had closed the email and packed Erik's things in several cardboard boxes, quickly, efficiently and numbly, still firmly in his Ice Queen mode.

The boxes sat stacked near the door of his apartment. He had a crazy desire to open them, to press his face to Erik's sweaters as if he was in the very worst melodramatic movie ever. He knew it was cheesy. He knew it was awful. But it didn't change the fact that at that moment, all he wanted to do was smell Erik, be surrounded by Erik, be near Erik. He just wanted Erik.

The tears continued; the lump in his throat was nearly choking him. He curled up on his bed, which no longer smelled like Erik, and cried. He just had to get it out, right? Just let it all out, all at once: missing Erik, missing his laugh, missing his smile, missing the feel of him in the night, missing the steadiness and the stable feeling he'd brought to Daniel's life. He just had to get it all out right now, and then Daniel could begin getting over him.

WE'RE SORRY TO SEE YOU GO, DANIEL.

Please consider taking a moment to answer a survey to help us best understand where we went wrong.

Your input is essential in making Aurora a more helpful app!

Good luck and all the best,
The Aurora Team

FOUR WEEKS AFTER ERIK LEFT, and two days after he'd uninstalled all the wedding-related apps on his phone and computer, Aurora had sent him an e-mail. Or rather, the website's registration database had sent him a form letter e-mail. It was a computer program, not a person, after all. It wasn't personal. Aurora didn't really care. Aurora didn't know, and couldn't know, where everything had gone wrong. Daniel didn't even know himself.

Most of the time, with his break-ups, he'd been able to convince himself it was for the best, and sometimes he required no convincing at all that he was better off without them, without their criticisms, without their ridiculous behavior and demands. Usually, that stage kicked in a few days after the break-up. The duration of Stage Two, which he was currently mired in, varied, but Stage Three—the "I Will Survive" angry and defiant stage—always kicked in, and this gray fog he was in would lift and everything would burn bright and hot and like shards of hyper-colored glass. He'd get in touch with his inner rebel, his inner spunk and gutsiness. He'd sing the Gloria Gaynor classic and any number of Cher songs and he'd feel so much better. He just had to survive this quagmire of dull aching and exhaustion until he got there.

Right now, he just missed Erik. He missed him, with a bone-deep pain. He missed his smell, and his laugh and his arms tight around him. He missed Erik's pragmatic, dry sense of humor, the deadpan delivery that had delighted Daniel once he'd gotten used to it. He missed his confidence, the certainty of him. Erik had a certain energy, a certain hum. When Erik was around, Daniel could feel the thrumming vibrations of him, even when he was absolutely silent.

Daniel snorted. He'd clearly spent too long with Carynne, if he was going to start crying about missing someone's cosmic vibrations. Then he sighed. Just because he thought it was ridiculous didn't mean it wasn't also true. He missed the hum of Erik. His apartment seemed far too empty without Erik's energy resonating in it.

The skin on his face was stretched tight and hot; the muscles around his eyes were beginning to cramp from all the crying. His nose burned from contact with the tissues. When he didn't give a second thought to giving up tissues and using the sleeve of his T-shirt to wipe the snot and tears off his face, he realized it was time to call Kate.

"Oh, honey." Her arms loaded with grocery bags, Kate smiled sadly at Daniel as he opened his door. "Oh, oh, oh, honey."

Daniel tried to smile, but he couldn't stop it wavering and gave up. He knew he looked awful. His eyes were swollen and red from crying, he had a runny nose and he was still in his pajamas. He shoved the tissue he'd just used on his nose in his already-full bathrobe pocket, shifted the tissue box to under his other arm and reached to take one of the grocery bags. "Hi, Kiki Dee."

"You were supposed to call me before Stage Two started. We agreed you would always call me *before* Stage Two," she scolded, refusing his help and pushing her way into his apartment. "You are a d. u. m. dumb bunny and you should have called me earlier."

Daniel trailed after her into the kitchen and watched her willowy frame bend as she slid the bags on the counter. "I know."

"You are a stupid, idiotic, ridiculous sobbing mess." She turned and held out her arms. "You're supposed to call me, so we can be stupid, idiotic, ridiculous sobbing messes *together*. Give me a hug, sugar."

He let himself be wrapped up in her arms, bending slightly to rest his head on her shoulder. "I love you, Keeks."

"I love you, too. Even when you're smearing snot in my hair." She sighed, rubbing his back. "It's going to be okay, Danny."

He was all cried out; there was nothing left inside him but a dull lassitude. His cheeks were stretched tight, and his nose was rubbed raw. "I don't think so, Kiki."

"You always say that. Remember Tommy Johnson when we were nine? When you broke his front tooth on the playground because he'd teased you? You didn't think it was going to be okay then, either." She gave him an extra squeeze and let him go. "And look how that turned out."

Daniel nodded, remembering. "My first boyfriend seven years later."

"And you're still good friends, right?" Kate turned and began unpacking the groceries. "You guys hang out, have a good time together."

"Yeah, I guess." Daniel sighed. "I mean, I haven't talked to him in a while, but yeah, Tommy's great."

"That's one disaster that turned out okay in the end."

"Sometimes, I wonder why I broke up with him," Daniel said wistfully. "My life would have been so different if I'd never broken up with Tommy after high school."

"Oh god, here we go again." Kate started unpacking the groceries. "Are you going to wax poetic about all your exes now? I thought we had to get some vodka in you before that started."

"No." Daniel sat down on the kitchen chair with a thump. "I can't remember them all."

"That's bullshit, but I am not going to push it because I really don't need to hear about your former flames and flings right now. Right now," she said as she pulled a pan from the cupboard, "we are making you dinner."

Daniel looked around. "I just ate breakfast."

"Danny, for Christ's sake, how long have you been holed up in here? When did he leave?"

"It was—he—" Daniel could feel the tightening in his throat, and cleared it roughly. "I'm not even sure."

"Oh, honey." She ran a hand over his hair. "You should have called me."

"Well, it didn't seem—I need to get through Stage One first, without you. Otherwise, I would have bit your head off, and you would have left me, too."

"I'm never going to leave you, you idiot, no matter how bitchy you get. I love you too much. Plus you're the only who gets me through my crazy life."

Daniel pressed his lips together and traced patterns on the tabletop with his fingertips. "You know what I mean."

"Yes, you feel all clear-headed and entirely convinced that it's not going to affect you, and you become a real bitch-ass bastard and truthfully, I kind of hate you when you're like that. I mean, I love you—always—but, Stage One Breakup Daniel is not really my idea of a good time."

"I'm sorry," Daniel said.

"Oh, don't be, honey." She lightly punched him in the shoulder. "I'm making you some chicken cacciatore, and while it cooks, I got you that ice cream you like—"

"That's so nice of you, Kiki." Tears overflowed, and he really wished he could stop them, but it was impossible.

"Oh, good lord, Danny." Kate shoved a tissue at him. "What are we going to do with you?"

"I don't know." Daniel stared at the table top as Kate set an ice cream pint in front of him.

"I brought all the usual movies. I wasn't sure what level of Stage Two we're at, so I just brought them all."

"I don't even know. I don't know what I'm doing. I don't know what's going on. I don't know, Kiki."

"Okay, honey. Why don't you go put a DVD in the machine while I start this simmering?"

"BUT, BY GOD, THERE WILL be dancing." Daniel recited the last line as the credits of *My Best Friend's Wedding* rolled. Two movies into their movie marathon, and both of them were decidedly drunk. "It's just like you and me, Keeks. That's just like you and me."

Kate held up her wineglass in a salute. "Yes, Danny. I mean, you are totally Julia Roberts and I will gladly accept being Rupert Everett. That man is hella gorgeous in that movie."

"Oh god, yes," Daniel agreed.

"I wasn't exactly sure about making you watch wedding stuff after all the shit that went down, but—"

"Oh, no." Daniel shook his head. "The 'you and me'-ness of it is just so perfect that I— I'm just really, really happy that you didn't try to break up my wedding because you'd never realized that you were in love with me, and I didn't get to marry Cameron Diaz after all."

"That doesn't make any sense." Kate giggled. "You're not making any sense. And I'm Rupert Everett, *you're* Julia Roberts. Julia tries to break up the wedding."

"Mostly, I'm just feeling really happy that I didn't have to plan any of that wedding. Those flower arrangements alone would have devastated our budget."

Kate snorted. "You're not making any sense. You're drunk, Danny."

"I'm not drunk. I'm just feeling so happy." Daniel slurred his words and sniffed loudly. "I mean, I'm just so grateful that I've got you as such a good friend."

"Uh-oh." Kate lightly tossed a box of Kleenex at him. "Is it waterworks time again, honey?"

"How did you know?" Daniel began to cry. "How do you always know exactly what I'm going through, Kiki? You're so good."

"You've been my best friend since third grade, honey. I just know."

"You just know." Daniel nodded sadly to the dregs of his ice cream and sighed.

"You know, I can't believe he actually left, Kiki." Daniel nearly sloshed his glass of wine into his ice cream bowl. "I—I knew he would, but I can't believe he actually did."

"I know."

"He didn't come back either. He just went to his conference and went straight on to his dig in Sweden and he didn't even come back."

"You pretty much told him not to, Danny." Kate finished scraping the bottom of her pint of ice cream. "As much as we'd love it to be, life is not a romantic comedy."

Daniel sighed. "I know. But it should be."

"He's a—he's a good guy. You told him you didn't want to be with him anymore, and he's going to respect that, you know? He's not going to come running down the street in the rain, or send you a million roses or anything like that. He's going to respect that you know your own mind well enough to know what you want and what you don't want."

"I just wish..." he trailed off as he reached for another chip. "I don't even know what I wish anymore."

"I know, honey." she sighed. "How are you feeling?"

"Sad," he said as he stared down into his ice cream. "Just really tired and sad and like everything is so fucking heavy. Just everything feels like such a problem and a chore and a hassle to get accomplished. I'm tired of lying down, but I don't have the energy to sit up, you know?"

"You want to watch another movie?"

"No. I don't know, maybe. I don't want to watch another one that's going to make me cry."

"*Robin Hood*?"

"The Disney one, yes. Though I feel kind of weird about being attracted to a fox." Daniel shrugged and swiped at his nose with a tissue.

"Me, too. But it's such a good movie."

"ANNIKA CALLED ME," DANIEL SAID as the next movie's credits ended.

Kate raised her head from the couch pillows. "And what did Fuckface have to say?"

"She said she was just checking up on me."

"She wanted to gloat," Kate glowered. "She wanted to rub it in."

"Probably."

"God, I wish I could rub her face on a—on a—on a something that's really awful." Kate shut one eye and reached out to grab her wine glass.

"Yeah, me too." Daniel got up, swayed and steadied himself before shuffling to the kitchen.

"Sometimes I wonder if she's got some secret tragic story." Kate belched. "If she's such a fuckface because she, like, lost her fiancé in a war, or was abandoned by her parents at a circus, or she has some other weird thing going on."

"I mean, obviously she's got *something* going on. But mostly, I think she just likes being a bitch."

"You mean, she's not going to show up on your doorstep in the rain and explain how sorry she is she never really accepted you and Erik together because she's been in love with him for such a long time, but now she's coming to terms with it and she wishes you well?"

"You watch too many fucking movies." Daniel bopped her lightly on the head as he shuffled back to his spot on the couch with a fresh pint of ice cream. Somehow, even now, he couldn't reveal what Erik had told him about Annika and her feelings for him. It didn't seem right to break his promise to Erik. "Things in real life don't get that much closure. Things don't get tied up in a little bow like that."

Huddled in the quickly dimming late August sunlight, Daniel sat on Kate's fire escape, balanced precariously on a slowly deforming plastic crate and staring moodily at the traffic on the expressway in the distance. It was almost peaceful sitting here in the dark, he mused. He kind of liked sitting here, all by himself. Thankfully, Stages Two and Three had passed relatively quickly, and he found himself in a Stage Four he'd never experienced: calm lassitude, a sense of dull serenity. No crying jags, no rebellious outbursts. He just *was*.

He'd been sitting out here long enough that the ice in the margarita Kate had pushed into his hand had completely melted.

Of course, with any party came the smokers, stepping out for a quick cigarette before the glowering silence on the fire escape chased them back inside. Daniel wordlessly handed them the lighter Kate kept stashed on the windowsill, murmured inconsequential platitudes at their awkward attempts at conversing with him and generally scowled enough to keep everyone's smoke breaks short.

It wasn't that he was avoiding going back inside and facing the vapid chatter of people he didn't particularly know or care for—Kate, excluded. It was just that he was avoiding going back inside and facing the vapid inane chatter of people babbling simply for the sake of babbling.

Two years ago, he would have been the life of the party, cracking jokes in the midst of the crowd, mixing drinks and chatting away with everyone. Gleefully making plans with everyone, plans that would always fall through. "Oh, we should go out. Oh, we should try that place. Oh, we definitely should get together."

But nobody really meant it, not the people currently dancing and drinking in Kate's apartment. Plans changed, phone numbers were lost, mindless excuses were made for false commitments, and so it was that this group of people rarely saw each other outside of parties.

Five years ago, he'd met Matthew here. Matthew, who had been coming off a bad breakup but wanted to get back in the game. Gorgeous Matthew, charming Matthew, wheedling and flirtatious Matthew. Daniel had been young and starry-eyed and overwhelmed that someone like Matthew would even be interested in talking to him.

Matthew who'd refused to say, "I love you" while they had sex, who'd made jabbing comments about Daniel's weight, his hair style, even his height, as if Daniel could suddenly grow three inches *if he really wanted to*. Matthew, who so clearly wanted Daniel to be someone else, and Daniel had been too blind to see that for far too long.

Matthew, who wanted Daniel to be less exuberant, more serious, less talkative, less artistic. Matthew who sneered when he spoke of Daniel's friends: "Freaky freaks" he called them.

Matthew, who was currently clambering his way out the window onto the fire escape with a sheepish, yet determined, look on his face.

Daniel's feet dropped to the fire escape floor with a dull metallic clang. He wiped his nose on his sleeve and stood abruptly, hoping to shove by him with a minimum of conversation or contact.

"Oh, you're leaving?" Matthew sounded surprised, and Daniel hated him for it.

"Yeah, I'm just gonna—" Daniel waved toward the party inside.

Matthew planted himself in the way. "I know you don't—I just— could you just wait a minute?"

Daniel could only glare at him.

"Look, I know, okay? I have no right to ask anything from you. I just—would you let me talk to you?"

Daniel leaned back against the railing with his arms crossed and raised his eyebrows. "Fine. But make it quick."

"Okay. Uh." Matthew seemed confused. Daniel squelched the desire to smooth over this awkwardness, to make it easier on Matthew as he had habitually done when they were together.

"I went—I was at St. Cecilia's the other day, to talk to Father Tim—" Daniel pursed his lips. "You did what, now?"

"Yeah, I know. I just—I've been doing a lot of thinking lately and I needed—I needed to talk to someone who wouldn't bullshit me. You always said he was a stand-up kind of guy."

"He is," Daniel said, then bit his lip to keep himself from supplying anything helpful to keep the conversation going. *Let the bastard roast in his own juices*, he thought. *He's earned some time being uncomfortable.*

Matthew laughed. "He's—he's a good guy. He really is. And we talked about who I am, where I'm going, what I'm doing. I went in there one day for just a quick chat, and wound up spending the entire afternoon, just babbling. Once I started talking, I couldn't stop. And he just sat there and listened and didn't say much at all."

Daniel shifted his weight and re-crossed his arms. "So you had a spiritual crisis and you talked to Father Tim for an afternoon and now you want me to do what with this information, exactly?"

"I—" Matthew said, biting his lip. "Look, I talked to him about my parents and my—my life and Layla and—and you."

"Me?"

"I wanted to ask him if I was—just how much of an asshole I am."

Daniel laughed, without humor. "And what did he have to say?"

"Pretty much, yes. I am a gigantic ass, a real jerk and an absolute fucking bastard, at least in regards to you."

"Father Tim did not say that."

"Well, no. Not those words, exactly. But, that's pretty much what he meant. He really let me have it, at first. He really cares about you. He's really protective of you."

Daniel snorted. He didn't know Father Tim as he'd known Father Brian, but Father Tim had become a friend in recent years. A former rugby player, he was built like a brick wall and had a fiery temper he worked very hard to control.

"Anyway. Yeah." Matthew scrubbed at the back of his neck. "Yeah, Father Tim is cool. We actually have a standing sort of thing, every other week."

"You're going to confession now?" Daniel sounded sarcastic and derisive and he was proud of himself for it.

"No, not, not confession. I just go there, and we talk about how things are going. It's kind of nice having someone who expects me to be a nicer person, you know? He makes me feel like I'm worth being a better person than I have been."

"Yeah." Daniel looked down at the fire escape. "Yeah, I know how that is."

"Anyway, Danny." Matthew smiled, genuine and boyish. "Father Tim showed me your window."

Daniel braced himself for Matthew's usual biting remarks.

"It's really beautiful, I mean, really. I didn't know—I didn't know you ever did stuff like that.

"You never bothered to find out."

"You're right. And I'm sorry, Danny. I'm so sorry."

"Now you're sorry?"

"I just—I wrote you off. I did. I didn't give you enough credit for, for anything, really. And I should have. I should have known."

Daniel scrubbed at his chin; he felt a lump in his throat.

"Believe me, Danny, I've met a lot of guys since we broke up, a lot of guys—"

"Spare me the details."

"—and none of them were anywhere near as kind and caring and funny as you—" Matthew continued as if he hadn't heard him.

"I'm going to stop you right here because this sounds like you're about to burst into tears and start the 'we should get back together' spiel, and I'm going to tell you right fucking now that that is not fucking going to happen."

"Give me some credit, Danny. I am not going there."

"Good." Daniel sniffed.

"I know when I've permanently fucked something up. I've had a great deal of experience at it."

"Oh, fuck off," Daniel snarled. "You always pull this martyr shit and it just is not going to fucking work on me again."

"No, you fuck off." Matthew smiled benignly.

"No, you," Daniel said, but his heart wasn't in it. As he had for months, he was more tired than upset. He was most likely losing a golden opportunity, the chance to tell Matthew every vicious thing Daniel had ever thought about him, every retort and rebuttal that Daniel kept locked in his head. But he was just so tired.

"So, I heard about that Reinholt job—my grandmother plays bridge with her. She said you've been doing beautiful work and she couldn't wait for you to get started on the rest of your designs. She's really happy with the windows you've done, and she said you took a leave of absence because you were sick. And I just, I got worried that you were really sick or something."

"I am not discussing my life with you. I don't even know why I'm still out here, listening to this crap."

"Please, just let me say this, and then I swear you never have to talk to me again. I promise."

Daniel watched the cars on the faraway expressway, wishing he could somehow be in one, speeding away from this conversation. "Fine. But make it quick."

"Look, she's worried about you. And Father Tim says you haven't come around to see him lately. And you just you don't look healthy, Danny. What's going on?"

"Did you not hear me when I said I wasn't discussing my life with you? I'm fine. I'm abso-fucking-lutely fine."

"Andre mentioned you'd been really seriously dating some guy but then that ended?"

"Andre needs to keep his mouth shut."

"Danny, I'm just, are you sick? Is it bad? Is that why he broke up with you?"

"I am not sick!" Daniel burst out, throwing his arms wide, unable to keep it in. "And I broke up with him, if you must know. And, what the hell does it matter to you, anyway?"

"I've been looking for patterns, you know? In my life. Patterns that repeat, and things that I might be able to change about them. And it makes me notice patterns in other people's lives."

"Have you been listening to Yanni a lot?" Daniel sneered. "New-age crystals and burning incense and all that crap? Because this sounds kind of like horseshit."

"You did this beautiful amazing window, really impressive profess-ional artistic stuff, when you were nineteen. Then, you kind of did not much for a long time. You started Co-Op, sure. But your art, you didn't really do much with that."

"I have no idea what you're trying to get at."

"When you were with me, you made crap, Danny. Sure, it was crap art that sold pretty well, but it still crap, and you know it."

"Fuck off."

"And then when you were with him, you started those amazing windows."

"If you use the word 'amazing' one more time, I might punch you in the dick. I'm just warning you."

"Danny, seriously." Matthew dismissed the threat with a shake of his head. "What was it?"

"It was him!" Daniel said. "Or... It was me when I was with him."

"What about him?"

"Well, he didn't make me feel like I was nothing, for one thing." Daniel narrowed his eyes at Matthew. "He made me feel important. And strong. And smart. And creative."

"He boosted your self-esteem."

"Yeah. And it was in serious need of boosting, thanks to you."

"I'm sorry, Danny."

Daniel shook his head, refusing to acknowledge the apology. "But more than that, he loved me. And he loved *me*, with all the crap that I do and all the baggage that I've got. He loved *me*."

Matthew nodded his head, looking as if he might be about to cry.

Daniel couldn't stop talking, letting it all barrel out of him. "He loved that we were so different. He loved that we didn't think about doing things the same way. He wanted me to be my own person; he loved it when I stood up for myself and did things on my own."

"He sounds like he was a great guy."

"He is," Daniel said, slumping a little. "He's a great guy. I mean, he can also be a complete asshole sometimes, but mostly he's a great guy."

"Why did you break up with him?"

"Do you have any idea how hard it is to be in love with someone when you're always arguing? He's neat, I'm not. He's organized, I'm not. He's punctual, I'm not."

"You're creative, he's not," Matthew supplied. "You're caring, he's not."

"No, no," Daniel shook his head. "He *is* creative. And he's really caring. It's just it's not as easy for him to show it to everyone."

"Unlike you, who's an open book."

"I'm much more flamboyant, and crazy and wild and yes, maybe I'm an open book. But he's—it's not that he doesn't care. He really cares very deeply. He's just more reserved about showing it. He doesn't wear his heart on his sleeve."

"Not like you," Matthew said softly. "You never had trouble showing people you care about them."

"Don't you dare start getting sentimental on me, Matty. Don't you dare."

"Yeah." Matthew laughed awkwardly. "Listen, I don't know, Danny. All I'm trying to say is that I care about you, and I'm worried about you, and that, you know, if Erik really was a bad deal for you, then that's that and you're better off without him."

"He wasn't a bad deal for me. He was very good for me. I'm sad and I'm upset and I miss him like hell, but I'm not destroyed now that we're not together. He helped me get up on my own two feet, and he didn't do anything to knock me down when we broke up—not like you."

"I know I deserve that. I do," Matthew said. "And I'm sorry."

"It's a little late for that."

"I know." Matthew looked out into the night that had finally fallen. "He sounds like a good guy to me."

"Well, your opinion matters so much to me, Matthew darling," Daniel sneered, but his heart wasn't in it.

"Is he still around?"

"He's in god-knows-where Sweden, at a dig site. And then he's teaching at a university, for the next year at least. I don't really have any way of getting in touch with him. I don't know if he's even checking his old email address, or if he'd answer me."

"Why wouldn't he check his old email address? That seems like a crazy thing not to do."

"Yeah, well. I don't know. I haven't tried to contact him." Daniel really wished he had a drink.

"You're afraid of how much it will hurt if he doesn't answer."

"Shut up, okay? Just shut up. Just because we're having this conversation right now does not mean that we're friends."

"Just one more thing, and then I'm leaving."

"Fine. Spill it and get the hell out of my way."

"Just because it's not perfect all the time, doesn't mean that it's not *right.*"

Daniel wanted to retort, wanted to say something biting. But he had to stop and think about that for a while. Nauseated, he wanted to sit down, anywhere but back on that milk crate.

"Look, I'm leaving now. I came because Andre said you might be here, and I hoped I might get a chance to talk to you, but Kate's seriously pissed that I'm here, so I'm just leaving. I just wanted to—I just wanted to talk to you this once, and say those things, and now I'm done, and I'm out of here and I promise I won't try to bug you or be friends or anything like that."

"Yeah," Daniel said softly. "Thanks, Matty. Thank you."

"Don't thank me. I'm just trying to be a better person."

"You need to come up with a new phrase for that. You sound like a broken record. But maybe you're making progress on it."

Matthew smiled and slipped back through the window without saying another word.

"DANNY!" GLORIA'S FACE LIT UP as she saw him walking up the concrete side path to St. Cecilia's the next day. "I was just heading home for lunch."

"Is Father Tim around?"

"No, honey, he's out visiting Mr. LaPierre." She sighed and took his arm. "He's not long for this world, I'm afraid."

"I'm sorry to hear that."

"I made cookies," Gloria said. "And chicken salad for sandwiches, if you'd like to join me for lunch."

"Anything for your cookies, Gloria." Daniel smiled down at her as they walked slowly across the green toward Gloria's house.

"Good. You need some fattening up, and I need to stop eating those cookies all by myself."

Daniel sat at Gloria's kitchen table; its Formica top was set with placemats and cloth napkins. She poured him a glass of milk, pulled the bread out of the breadbox and began making their simple lunch.

Her kitchen smelled of apple cider and coffee, warm and wholesome. It was the smell he remembered from visiting her here as a child; it never changed in all the years he'd been here. It was soothing and homelike, and he breathed it in deeply.

"Now, honeyface, what's your trouble?" she asked as she set the plate down in front of him.

"I just—I don't know, Gloria. I just feel like—"

"Something's gone wrong and you don't know how to fix it?"

"I, I mean, things are going great right now, you know? Things are fine. Work is fine, my life is fine."

"'Fine,' huh?" She settled herself in her chair around the corner from him.

"Yeah, fine." Daniel frowned at his sandwich, which was cut in half on the diagonal, just as he liked.

"Eat," Gloria prodded. "You look peaked."

Daniel took a bite of his sandwich. They ate in silence.

"Now, Danny." She put down the last of her own sandwich. "Tell me about Erik."

"What about Erik?"

"I know you two broke up, I have gathered that he left town directly afterward. But I haven't heard how you're doing."

"I'm doing great," Daniel insisted. "Everything's fine."

"Daniel," she chided. "Tell me."

"There's nothing to tell, Gloria."

"Honeyface, that's just not true. Tell me why it ended."

Daniel leaned his elbows on the table and stared at his plate. *Why did it end?*

"For a million reasons, Gloria," he said impatiently. "I can't go into them all."

"Then tell me just one." Gloria wiped her lips with her napkin. "And before you do that, go get the cookie jar, there's a dear."

Daniel grabbed the cookie jar from the sideboard and held it, considering. "I thought being in love would be like that couple I read about in *People* magazine, you know? Married sixty years and they write each other love notes every single day and never have an argument."

"Oh please, that's just bullshit."

"Gloria!" Daniel gasped.

"Oh, give me a break. There's no church service going on." Gloria frowned at him.

"I can't remember if I've ever heard you talking like this—"

"Well, pardon my French, but your *People* magazine idea is just utter horseshit. Maybe those people wrote each other love notes but they were secretly hating each other every single day. Maybe she was screwing the milkman. Maybe *he* was screwing the milkman. Maybe they were both dead inside. Maybe they're both idiots."

Daniel sat down with the cookie jar. "I just wanted it to be... perfect, you know? I didn't want to end up like my parents."

"Honey," she said, looking at him over her glasses, "you are not either one of your parents. You've got your father's nose and—God bless him—his idiot grin. You've got your mother's elbows. The rest of you, baby boy, is all you."

"I've got my mother's elbows?" Daniel twisted his arm to try to look at them.

"Can it, and cut the crap, smartass." Gloria fished cookies out of the jar and dropped them on the plate in front of him. "Eat."

"Gloria, this is the most I've ever heard you swear." Daniel took a cookie and broke it into pieces.

"Well, you've got your head in your ass, but it's time to pick yourself up by your bootstraps and come to Jesus."

"The imagery of that is just mind-boggling." Daniel shook his head and crumbled the cookie into smaller and smaller pieces.

"And now you're trying to change the subject." Gloria sat in the corner chair, close enough to reach out and poke him sharply in the arm. "We're talking about you and how you need to shake things up. Go out and see people. Do things."

"I do do things." Daniel swiped cookie crumbs briskly off the table into his hand. "I do see people."

"To start with, Mrs. Greenbaum told me that Marjorie Walker told her that Phillip Brushkin saw you flirting with Charlie Stanfield outside the Whole Foods the other day." Gloria looked at him over the top of her glasses. "Now, schtupping Charlie Stanfield silly on a regular basis may be your idea of a good time—"

"Christ, Gloria," Daniel muttered. "I'm not schtupping Charlie."

"—But I've known both you boys since you were born and I can tell you Charlie Stanfield is not the man who's going to make you happy."

"Gloria, I'm not—"

"Don't interrupt me, Danny." She scowled at him. "I'm an old woman, and I've earned the right to give you advice whenever I feel like it. The Lord knows how much advice I had to listen to when I was your age."

Danny started to interrupt, thought better of it, and instead made a show of shoving a piece of cookie in his mouth. Gloria chuckled and continued.

"Charlie Stanfield is a good boy, and he's built like his grandfather, so I bet he's hung like a horse on a brass maypole—"

Daniel choked on the cookie.

"I can see the attraction of that, Danny, I really can. I remember when I lost my first husband, sixty years ago, how nice it was to go out with a nice man, have a nice dinner, have a nice screw and just go to sleep. No worries, no fuss, no big deal. It was just nice to be wanted again, even for just a little while."

"Gloria, did you sleep with Charlie's grandfather sixty years ago?"

She looked at him sternly. "We're not talking about me. We're talking about you."

"You can't just drop these facts on me and not expect me to wonder about you and Mr. Stanfield and horses with brass dicks."

"We'll talk about George Stanfield and his brass dick later. Right now, you twit, we're discussing you."

"Me…"

"Look, honey. It's okay to take some time, and lick your wounds. It's okay to just let yourself float for a little while, to let yourself heal. But it's not okay to let yourself stagnate."

"I'm not stagnating! I'm working! I'm going out!"

"You're going out with Charlie Stanfield, who may have a brass-horse dick like his grandfather, but the boy is mellow to the point of being comatose."

"I'm not seeing Charlie!" Daniel protested. "And even if I was, Charlie's a sweet guy."

"Oh, I know that, honey. He's a sweet, sweet boy, who never says 'boo' to anyone. He doesn't have two thoughts to rub together most days. He's sweet and harmless and never argues. I bet he's a real blast in bed."

"He's a good guy."

"I never said he wasn't, Danny. But he's not who you need."

"You want me to go out and see people, just not Charlie, huh?" Daniel laughed. "So, who do I need, Gloria?"

"You need someone to keep your brain busy. You need someone to fight with. You need someone who's just as nasty and awful as you think you are sometimes. You need someone who's going to inspire you to do better."

"To do better—what am I doing now?"

"You're letting yourself be happy just getting by. You're not challenging yourself; you're just being a shell of yourself. It's okay to be that, for a while, while you heal, but you always need to keep the real you in sight. Keep you as a goal."

"I'm not just getting by, Gloria," Daniel protested. "I'm challenging myself."

"That is also horseshit." Gloria smoothed out the placemat in front of her. "I walked into your Co-Op the other day, and what of your beautiful art do I see? I see bullshit sun-catchers. I see boring, pedestrian, bullshit work. It was art that anyone could have done. There wasn't a single thing in there that said to me, 'Danny made this.'"

"Well, maybe I just—maybe I just haven't felt up to doing any non-bullshit work, Gloria." Daniel knew he would get in trouble for his sass, wasn't surprised when Gloria brought her hand sharply down on his.

"There was a Barney sun-catcher in there, Daniel Seagram Whitcomb." She glared at him over her glasses while holding his hand tightly so tightly he could feel her rings biting into his fingers. "That god-awful devil spawn purple dinosaur. In a sun-catcher."

"It was supposed to be ironic."

"There were two of them, Daniel. You made two goddamned Barney sun-catchers. I don't care if you thought you were being a smartass; you're wasting your time on that. You're capable of so much more."

Daniel stared at the cookie crumbs on the table in front of him and pushed them slowly around with one finger. Gloria kept a tight hold of his other hand.

"Why'd you break up with him, honeyface?" she asked. "Why'd you end it with Erik?"

Daniel sighed. "It was just too hard. Planning a wedding, and he was moving to Sweden for a year, and it was just—it was too hard. We argued all the time, about everything. It was exhausting."

"But good, sometimes, right?"

"Yeah." Daniel paused. "Yeah, it was good, sometimes. It was fucking great sometimes."

"Were those good times enough for you?" Gloria asked. "Enough to balance out the differences?"

"I don't know. It felt like it would have been easier if we were more alike. If I had someone more like me. If he'd been more affectionate, more open, more… crazy, like me. It just felt like it should have been easier, you know? Being in love should have been easier."

"Honeyface, falling in love is easy. Staying in love is the trick."

"Gloria, you sound like a greeting card." He smiled.

"Where do you think the greeting cards get it from? Old people, like me. Steal it right out from our mouths and we don't see a penny." She slapped his hand several times, light and loving. "Now, sweetcheeks, what are you going to do?"

Daniel shrugged. "I don't know, Gloria. I thought things were going okay. I don't know if I need to do anything different."

"Daniel, make an old woman happy. Go out and do something that will make your life better. Stretch yourself. Grow. Do something that frightens you."

"You want me to go rock-climbing? Or what?"

"Don't be an asshole, Daniel," she chided. "Just go do something new, okay? Do it for me. Change your day."

DANIEL RUTHLESSLY BEGAN CLEANING OFF his desk; he couldn't remember the last time he had done it. It was piled high with stuff. Magazines he thought he'd definitely want to read—later. Paperwork he'd need to file—later. Sketches of work to be done—later. Things he didn't have any use for now, but thought he might—later.

It was a sunny day in late in August and "later" had finally arrived. He dragged the recycling bin over, grabbed a pile of things and sat on the floor sorting through the detritus. Could it really have been more than a year since he'd last cleaned off his desk?

Paid bills got their own manila folders. Another file for important paperwork he wasn't quite sure what to do with. Seeing the files hanging in his new cabinet, he felt responsible and grownup and slightly smug.

He'd bought a brand-new artist's folio in case there were some designs worth saving in this pile of crap. He found a few important papers, a lot of papers to be recycled, three pencil sharpeners, four erasers and that set of watercolor pencils he'd bought and promptly misplaced.

He also found a copy of *Archaeology Digest* Erik had left. At the sight of it, his stomach dropped, but only slightly. That was a definite improvement. He put the magazine off to the side. Maybe he'd figure out what to do with it later.

Halfway through the cleaning, he found one of Erik's pulp magazines, a duplicate copy of the issue containing Erik's favorite story: the one about Professor Schleissinger and the missing Tryptometric Filotron machine. He resisted the urge to sit there on the floor and reread it. Instead, he placed it carefully on his bookshelf, on top of some of his larger art books, flat and where it wouldn't be faded by the sunlight.

There were sketches. Some were awful, some good and a couple he definitely wanted to try to expand further. Matthew and Gloria had been right: He'd been playing it safe with his glasswork. He was bored with sun-catchers and lampshades, but maybe he'd expand his dabbles with jewelry.

He was not prepared to find a sheet of paper scribbled in Erik's nearly illegible handwriting: things lined out and rewritten. It was obviously his notes on something. Daniel sighed and was about to put it off to the side with the magazine he'd maybe someday return to Erik, when he saw his own name on the sheet.

It was Erik's vows. Or, at least an initial draft of them. Daniel felt the wind knocked out of him. He should put the paper away, out of reach with that magazine. Or maybe he should burn it, shred it, tear it up into tiny pieces—do anything but read it.

Daniel Seagram Whitcomb, today is the day that I officially pledge to be your husband, to love you and support you in your successes and your failures, to stand with you at your side through everything life throws at us. I'm officially pledging to it today, even though I had already signed on for spending the rest of my life with you about five minutes after I met you. You're it, for me. You're everything I never knew I wanted in a partner.

Before I met you, my life was well-ordered, logical and tidy. I didn't need to remind anyone to put their socks in the laundry hamper, or show them how to fold a shirt so it fits in the drawer without wrinkling, or remind them to eat dinner. I was happy.

You came into my life, and you brought chaos and color and energy and creativity. You've turned my world upside down. You showed me what I'd been missing. You are what I'd been missing. I was happy before I met you, but now that you're in my life, I know what joy feels like. You're not perfect, and neither am I, but we are perfect for each other. You're not my other half; you're what is keeping me balanced. You're my exact counterweight. You pull me up out of the depths and you anchor me when I soar too high.

I promise to love you, no matter what. Whatever happens in our life, I will love you until the day I die. I promise...

The rest of the page was blank, so Daniel didn't know what else Erik had thought about promising. His cold hands shook as he read over it again.

DANIEL KNEW IT WAS RIDICULOUS, but a lifetime of watching John Hughes movies had left him with the moderate certainty that he would arrive at his destination, find Erik with absolutely no trouble and sweep him away with declarations of love and devotion. They'd be reunited within a matter of hours.

He'd bought the airplane ticket to Stockholm, only choking a little bit on the price, which was a sad drop in the bucket of the wedding debt he was swimming in. He called Kate from the taxi and was thankful it went straight to her voicemail.

"Kiki, I'm, I'm going to get him back. My flight lands in Stockholm tomorrow night, I've got a horrific layovers but I've just—I've got to get him back. I don't know when I'll be home or anything, but I'll let you know how things are going. Don't worry." He had time to squeak two kisses before the beep cut him off.

He'd thrown clothes into a carry-on bag. According to the app on his phone, the weather would be variable, but he reasoned Stockholm was a fully functioning city and he could probably buy anything he really needed. He dragged the bag out of the taxi and into the international departures area and was thankful he'd at least remembered to grab his passport.

He got through security and found his gate when the plane was just beginning to board. He was on his way to Erik, to the love of his life, and he couldn't keep the smile off his face as he handed over his boarding pass.

He settled in his seat, a window seat miraculously still available at the last minute, and stashed the book he'd grabbed off his nightstand in the seatback pouch. It wasn't until the flight attendant started the safety demonstration, reminding the passengers to switch off their cellphones, that he suddenly remembered Erik talking about how his American cellphone hadn't worked in Europe.

Well, Daniel would have to figure that out.

He fell into a strange state he could only describe as non-awake: never fully asleep, never fully awake. He gave up trying to sleep when the flight attendants brought around large cups of potent coffee and began serving breakfast.

His first connection was in Amsterdam, where he had seven hours to wait. He spent some of them watching a group of college students, obviously fresh off a night-in-Amsterdam bender, trying to appear sober enough to board their plane. He settled in with a large coffee and some junk food and couldn't tell if the jitters roiling his stomach were from too much caffeine and sugar, or impatience with getting to Erik.

He arrived at the Stockholm airport and followed the crowd to the tourist office. He waited in line, poking through the racks of brochures, thinking it might be fun to go to the ABBA museum with Erik. He hoped someone behind the counter could help him find an inexpensive hotel, a bus to Erik's dig site and a bathroom, preferably not in that order.

"And can you tell me how I would get to Gotland?" He gathered up the information the smiling woman behind the desk had given him so far. "My fiancé—boyfriend—uh, my friend is working at the archaeological school there."

"Gotland?" She chuckled. "Yes. Let me find you the ferry information. When were you thinking of going?"

"Tonight." His confident smile faltered. "Did you say 'ferry?'"

"I'm sorry, but tonight won't be possible. It's a three-hour ferry ride. Or you could catch a flight, but I believe the last one has left."

Well, so much for John Hughes and being reunited within hours.

"Can you—" he swallowed hard. "Can you help me find a cheap hotel, instead? Just for tonight?"

She smiled at him. "Of course, sir." She pulled out a map and made a small "x" on it. "My sister-in-law's nephew stayed at this one a few weeks ago. He said it's very comfortable and not too expensive. And there's a grocery store next door, so you can buy anything you might need for your travel."

"Will they speak English?"

"Of course. Let me show you how to get there."

A few minutes later, tickets in hand, he found himself descending into a brilliantly lit but cavernous subway station. He stared at the wall, trying to decide if it was blackened and scary on purpose, or just an unhappy byproduct of underground construction, when his train arrived and he got on.

He found his way to the hotel with only a few moments of panic at not understanding any of the language spoken around him, checked in, sank into a comfortable bed and slept without even taking off his shoes.

The next morning, he double-checked the directions with the front desk clerk, who listened and nodded and added a few helpful pointers to help him get to the archaeological school. He bought snacks to take on the ferry, grabbed a bottle of suntan lotion so he wouldn't burn to a crisp if he had to sit outside on the boat and was on his way.

Once at the school, he found himself pouring his whole story out to a bus driver, Oskar, who smiled and nodded and said he could take the bus out to the dig site. One of the students milling around the entrance confirmed that Erik was there right now, with a group of students. He offered him another cup of coffee. How much coffee did the average Swedish person drink on an average day? He was soon crammed into the bus with a bunch of rather dusty, very chatty students, and they bounced their way out of the parking lot.

Daniel tuned out their chatter. As he looked out the window and watched the scenery go by, he was overwhelmed with an uneasy feeling. It was so impulsive of him to come here, possibly even rash. Maybe Erik wouldn't be happy to see him. A knot began to burn in the pit of his stomach. He wished he were calm, but his hands wouldn't stop shaking.

When they arrived at the dig site near the beach, the students clambered out of the van, still chatting. A brisk wind blew off the ocean, rustling the stands of trees at the far end of a meadow. A short girl with her T-shirt sleeves rolled up onto her shoulder pointed out where Erik was likely to be: a clearing just visible through the trees. Daniel thanked her and marched off in that direction

The deep rectangular holes in the ground in which the archaeology team worked were scattered randomly across the clearing. Daniel picked his way around them carefully. He didn't see Erik anywhere, and when he stopped to ask people where Erik might be, everyone shrugged and pointed him in a different direction.

"Daniel?" A voice he recognized called from one of the dig pits. "Is that you?"

Oh fuck. Annika. He watched her climb a ladder out of the pit, mutter to the group of students she was clearly overseeing and wipe her blond hair out of her eyes with the back of her dirty wrist.

"What are you doing here?"

"Uh." He gulped. "I'm here to see Erik?"

"Why the fuck are you here, Daniel?" She narrowed her eyes at him, pointing her dirt-crusted index finger at him. "Haven't you fucked him up enough?"

"I... I want to... to talk to him about all that." Daniel felt a surge of defiance. "It's really nice that you're such a good friend to him, but you know, it's really between me and him."

"Look, it's no secret that I don't like you—"

"No, I've never had any ideas otherwise—"

"You're completely wrong for him, you know that, right? You're exactly the opposite of what a man like Erik needs."

Daniel didn't want to let on how much it hurt to hear that.

"You know what, Annika? It sounds like you're trying to keep Erik for yourself."

"Fuck you, Whitcomb." Her eyes narrowed again. "I'm not in love with Erik, but even I'd be better for him than you'd be."

"Yes, a perfect relationship, you and him. Until he's desperate to have a dick in his mouth, that is. That's something you just can't provide, no matter how perfect you think you are." It was reckless, aggressive and bold, but Daniel couldn't stop himself.

"If you really care about Erik, you will turn around right now and leave before he sees you. Never ever try to contact him again."

"You understand that I really don't give a fuck what you think, right, Annika?" Daniel rolled his eyes.

"Umm, Annika?" A voice called hesitantly from the pit behind them. "I'm so sorry to bother you, but I think we've found something? And we need you to—"

"Yeah, I'll be right there," she snarled. She glared at Daniel one more time, shoving her fingertip into his chest. "Get the fuck out of here."

"Yeah, I'll get right on that," Daniel let his voice drip with sarcasm. He turned and walked farther into the dig site. He could feel Annika's eyes on him; most likely she wished she had the power to make him drop dead instantly.

Well, that was a small blemish on what still had the potential to be an incredible day. Daniel tried to shake it off, to let her opinion of him just roll off his shoulders. He stopped at the next person he saw to ask for directions to where he might find Erik.

"You're looking for whom?" A young man squinted up, still crouched down over the small square of dirt he was working on.

"Erik. Erik Kappel." Daniel smiled. "Do you know where I might find him?"

"And you are?" The young man raised his eyebrows and pursed his lips.

"Uh." Daniel was taken aback. Everyone else here had been so friendly and welcoming and helpful, he wasn't quite sure how to take this young man's attitude. "I'm Daniel. I'm a, a friend of Erik's."

The young man snorted. "Oh, I see. Well, I think he's taking his lunch break. He's probably in those trees."

"Thanks." Daniel turned to go.

"If I were you, I'd make a lot of noise while you're walking." The man almost sounded as though he was laughing.

"Yeah, thanks." Daniel set off, nervous and excited and cold all over. He walked and walked, until the sounds of the dig site faded behind him. He wanted his first words to Erik to be smart and eloquent, but he couldn't remember anything he'd wanted to say. He hadn't really pictured what he'd have to say, just that he'd say something brilliant and compelling, and Erik would agree they were meant to be together, and somehow everything would work out all right in the end.

He certainly didn't picture stumbling upon Erik leaning against a tree with a tall hulking blond man holding both his shoulders, with their foreheads pressed together. He could just barely see the look of searing longing on Erik's face, as the blond man spoke to him urgently in words Daniel couldn't hear.

Daniel felt as if he couldn't breathe, as if he might throw up on the spot. Of course, Erik had moved on. Of course he had. Erik was too amazing to be alone. Erik was too gorgeous and smart and everything Daniel ever wanted. This was such a terrible, awful and stupid idea, coming here, just exactly what Daniel should have expected from one of his plans. He'd have to be an idiot not to realize that it wouldn't work out. Why would he think that it would?

Daniel backed away, his breath sounding harsh and ragged, trying not to step on a stick or some other ridiculous thing that Erik and his new gorgeous Viking boyfriend might hear and be interrupted. Dizzy and exhausted, he trudged across the dig site to where the van had left him off. He sat on ground at the base of a tree, pulled his knees up to his chest and wrapped his arms around them and dropped his head. He tried very, very hard not to think.

Life really isn't the way it is in the movies.

He wasn't sure how much later, but he heard the crunching of gravel under boots. Looking up, he recognized a girl he'd seen earlier.

"Did you find Erik?" she asked cheerfully. She chugged water out of a bottle that dripped with condensation.

"Yeah, I—" he cleared his throat. "He was, um, really busy, so I'll just catch him later, or something."

Or, hopefully, never again. How could he could get out of this situation without Erik seeing him? Maybe someone would be leaving the site soon, perhaps heading in the general direction of the ferry dock, so he could finish this stupid, idiotic, ridiculous trip as soon as he possibly could.

"Mind if I sit?" The girl pointed to a spot in the shade near him.

"Sure, go ahead." He smiled what he hoped was brightly.

"Man, there's so much to do here. It's so awesome," she chattered away. "I'm just so pumped to be here, you know?"

"Yeah, it looks great." Daniel studied the ground near the heels of his boots, hiding his face.

"And Erik's such a great guy, you know?" she said as she drank more water. "He's not only an awesome teacher, but he's just so nice, too."

"Mm-hmm." Daniel didn't trust himself to say anything more.

"Hey!" She said excitedly. "There he is! Erik!"

"Oh god, no." Daniel felt a rush of horror, watching the girl frantically waving her arm to get Erik's attention. "Really, you don't have to—"

"Erik! Your friend's here!" she called.

Everything seemed to drag. Daniel saw Erik turn when he heard the girl's voice, saw him start to smile at her. Then he saw the moment Erik realized who was sitting on the ground next to her. Erik's face dropped; a look of surprise replaced the genial smile. A flush, perhaps of embarrassment, or maybe of guilt, and then another smile that Daniel couldn't read.

"Daniel," Erik said, walking over slowly, looking tired with shaggier hair and dark smudges under his eyes. He brushed dust off the front of his jacket, which was clearly new, clearly a replacement for the jacket he'd left at Daniel's house. "Hi."

"Hi," Daniel said cheerfully. He didn't want to think more about Erik's new jacket that replaced the battered old one Daniel had brought carefully folded in his suitcase. He stood up awkwardly, brushing the dust from the seat of his pants.

"How's it going?" He wanted to smack himself on the forehead. *What a stupid, idiotic thing to say.*

Erik frowned. "I'm okay. And you?"

"I'm doing great." Daniel smiled and nodded. "Really, really great."

"He said he was here to talk to you," the girl offered. "He looked like he might puke on the ride over here, too. I don't know, man, I think he might be dehydrated or something."

"Thanks, Reia." Erik smiled at her. "He and I will go find some water, I think."

"That's a good plan, dude." She capped her own bottle, bouncing up and smiling. "The sun is majorly brutal today."

They watched her walk off; her boots crunched in the gravel as she went. Daniel desperately tried to think of something, anything, to say.

"So," Erik began.

"Yeah, so." Daniel took a deep breath. He forced a bright smile on his face. "Surprise!"

"I think I need a drink," Erik said, and marched off toward a nearby tent.

Am I supposed to follow him? Daniel trailed behind. Erik opened one of several coolers on the floor and dug through the slushy ice water inside and came up with two bottles of water.

It wouldn't be like Erik to take two bottles of water and *not* offer one to Daniel, but Daniel didn't want to presume—he'd already done so much of that, and look where it had landed them. He hesitated until Erik shoved a bottle at him.

"Drink it," Erik said gruffly. "Reia's right; it's easy to get dehydrated out here, and we've already had to take two people to the hospital for heat stroke."

Daniel twisted open the bottle, drank in large gulps and then trailed the damp bottle over his hot, tight skin.

"So," Erik said.

"So, I—" Daniel began again. "I just—I wanted to talk to you about something."

"Okay." Erik started walking, heading toward the treeline and out of the direct sun. "So, talk."

"I…" Daniel didn't even know where to begin as he followed Erik out of the tent. Thoughts of covering this up flooded his mind; how easy it would be to make up a wild story about his parents having airline miles that had to be used, or needing the Wi-Fi password for the apartment, or something, *anything* other than the reason he was actually here; anything that would let him slink away to lick his wounds in private. He'd call Kate to stock up on booze and ice cream, and she could meet him at the airport when he landed. He could probably start drinking as soon as he got on the airplane, and maybe not stop for the next few days.

Erik was still glancing at him as they walked. None of those excuses were going to work.

Daniel took a deep breath and swallowed hard. Once they got into the trees, he stopped in the middle of the path. "I was cleaning off my desk and I found your vows. Or what were going to be your vows. Or your first draft of your vows, I don't know. The point is that I found them. And I, I kind of wondered if you still felt like that. And I just wanted to ask you in person, so I decided to be completely stupid and come all the way here to ask you, but then I got here and I found you, and you were with that guy, and I realized that of course you don't still feel like that. I've fucked up everything too badly to fix it, and you've moved on with a completely gorgeous guy who probably appreciates you and loves you and is smart and funny and brilliant and interesting, and I—"

He had to stop himself. His voice was rising in hysteria; it was only a matter of moments before he burst into tears.

Daniel took a deep, calming breath. It didn't work. "I'm sorry. I just—"

"You babble when you get nervous and upset," Erik said. "I know this."

"Right. I am really kind of nervous right now. And also feeling kind of dumb. But, you know what? Just never mind, okay? Like, we can just pretend none of this happened and I'll catch a ride back to the ferry and be out of your hair, and we can just forget all this ever happened, okay?"

Daniel plastered his most competent, genial nothing-is-wrong smile on his face. "It's totally nothing, okay? I did my usual ridiculous, impulsive thing, without thinking things through at all and I made a complete error in judgment coming here and I'm so sorry to bother you. I'm just gonna go find Oskar and see if he can give me a ride, or something."

"Danny." Erik put his hand out and took Daniel by the wrist. The lump in Daniel's throat tightened, and tears sprang to his eyes.

"Please, don't try to be nice right now." Danny wrinkled his nose and tried not to cry. "Just, don't. Okay? Let's just forget this, okay?"

"Don't do that, Danny. Don't try to run away. Let's talk about this." Erik said as he let go of Daniel's wrist.

"I'm sorry." Daniel licked his lips and continued in a rush, his words tumbling out in a torrent he couldn't have stopped even if he wanted to. "I know that I, I was so afraid that you were going to leave me that I never really committed to this, to you and me. I was always ready to run at the first sign of trouble because it's so much easier that way. It's so much easier if I'm the one who leaves first; it hurts so much less. And I'm so sorry for being like that. I'm really ready to start *not* being like that."

Daniel sniffed loudly. "And I'm, I'm just—I'm ready for this. I want to work it out. I want it to be you and me against the world. I want to argue and yell and fight and be happy and love each other for the rest of our lives. It's going to be awful sometimes, and it's going to be amazing sometimes, and I just want to be the person you rely on. I want you to be the person *I* rely on. I want us to be so certain of each other that it never enters our minds again that one of us will leave the other. I want to commit to that, that we're not leaving each other, ever."

Erik turned his head to stare down the path. "Come take a walk with me?"

Erik was often stoic and chillingly calm, but Daniel really couldn't tell what to expect, which made him even more nervous. They walked along the sun-dappled path; the breeze blew more strongly. The trees abruptly ended at a deserted rocky beach. Erik took his hand and marched him to a solitary windblown tree and sat down next to it, still silent.

Daniel squashed the urge to keep babbling, to talk and talk until he was certain Erik would agree with him, to keep going until all his anxiety was talked out, no matter what Erik thought or needed. Here was a chance to start again, to try to give Erik the space he needed to think and be, without Daniel hounding him to keep talking. Daniel pressed his lips together tightly.

"The thing is, I can't forget this, Danny." Erik voice was low and hoarse. "I can't forget you, no matter how hard I try. And I don't even think I really want to. I don't want to ever forget you."

Daniel bit his lip.

"You haven't forgotten me?"

Erik smiled. "I haven't forgotten you. I'm in love with you."

"Still? Really?"

"Really. Still." Erik tugged on his arm, pulling Daniel into his arms. "I'm going to need some time to get my head back together, maybe. It's been hard not having you and it's going to take some getting used to, for both of us, I think. But, Danny, yes. I'm still in love with you and I want to be with you and I want us together again."

Daniel sighed heavily; the tension rolled off him like a huge weight and he melted into Erik. He could finally breathe again.

"How did you get here?" Erik chuckled. "And just—why now?"

"Three planes, a bus, a ferry and a van full of college kids." Daniel sniffed, toying with Erik's hand. "As for why now, I just—I found your vows and it was like I heard a voice saying, 'You need to go to him.' So I did. I bought the first plane ticket that I could find and I threw things in a bag and I grabbed my passport, and I went to the airport. I didn't even tell Kate. I left her a message when I was in the taxi."

"You know she's going to kill you." Erik kissed Daniel's forehead.

"Yeah, probably. But she'll get over it. I think. Maybe." Daniel was struck by how good it felt to Erik back in his arms, how normal this felt, how regular and natural and unforced it was to be with him.

"So, you're not in love with Thor?"

"Thor who?" Erik's voice was muffled against Daniel's cheek as he held him tightly.

Daniel took a deep hitching breath, not quite ready to let go of him. He wasn't sure, yet, how much of what he saw bothered him. "The guy you were kissing in the bushes on your lunch break."

Erik froze, but didn't let go. Finally, he said, "Lars. Not Thor."

Daniel pulled back, sniffed and shook his head. "I didn't mean his name was really Thor. I meant he's tall and blond and gorgeous and like a Norse god, or something. I didn't—"

"I didn't, Danny. It's not a—" Erik stammered, as if he hadn't heard. He pulled away, sitting up abruptly. "I don't know if it matters, but I didn't kiss him first, he kissed me. He was just trying to help. I was lonely and so goddamned hurt; I've been shutting everyone out and— I don't want to upset you or hurt you, but it's really not a big deal and I need you to understand that he's really just my friend, and it's not a romantic thing, not really."

"Erik—" Daniel began.

Erik interrupted him. "No, Daniel, please let me just say this. I didn't think you'd ever come back to me, I thought I'd never see you again, and I—I kissed him back. I would have let it go further. I would have slept with him. I just wanted to feel something, Danny, just feel *anything*. I've been so—"

"Hey, baby, hush. Now *you're* babbling when you get nervous." Daniel reached out to take Erik's hand again. "I understand. Really, I do. We weren't together. We'd broken up. You weren't cheating on me, and I know that."

Erik let out a breath that was almost a sob.

"Aside from which, I would have kissed someone else, too, if I'd had the chance. All the guys I met were clearly more trouble than they were worth, and the only one who might have been a possibility, Gloria would have skinned me alive for kissing."

"We can talk through it, right?" Erik asked.

"We can talk about it. We can argue about it. We can have a fight about it, if you want, so long as you promise we're in this together, forever."

"Danny, that's all I've ever wanted. You and me against the world."

"Good," Danny sighed happily, pulling Erik into his arms and settling back more comfortably against the tree. "Except I have to tell you that the only fight I think we'll be able to have about the whole Thor thing is how much more attractive your Thor is than the guy Gloria was afraid I was dating. Thor is hot, man."

"His name is Lars. And, no, I am not interested in sharing you."

"You do understand that I don't really think his name is Thor, right? It's a joke."

"His brother's name is Thor."

"Seriously?"

"Seriously."

Daniel started to laugh, and Erik joined in.

◻

DANIEL STAYED WITH ERIK AT the Institute for eleven days, long enough to figure out his flights home, long enough to get several phone calls from a shrieking and excited Kate, long enough to begin getting comfortable with one another again. They fell into a wonderful routine. Each night, they tangled themselves together on Erik's tiny bed in the room he'd been assigned in the Institute's dormitory. Each morning, Daniel slept like the dead, and Erik quietly slipped out early for work. Erik came back at midday, dusty and grinning, and Daniel coaxed him to spend a few extra "private" minutes in their room before joining him in the dining hall for lunch.

Daniel rode the van with him in the afternoon, back to the dig site with everyone hollering and laughing, and spent the afternoon watching Erik teach his young students proper techniques and hooting with excitement whenever anyone found something. He sat in the shade of the trees at the edge of the site and sketched design ideas, or landscapes, or just Erik. Erik serious and concentrated on a task. Erik laughing and joyful and relaxed. Erik walking toward him at the end of the day with a smile on his face meant only for Daniel.

Erik's semester ended in January, and they hoped Daniel could fly back to spend Christmas with him in Sweden. For the moment, they savored their time together and lived in the moment.

◻

WHEN DANIEL RETURNED FROM TALLENBURG, he and Erik established another routine. It was hard with Daniel being six hours behind Erik's time zone. They could catch each other late at night for Erik, which was early in the morning for Daniel, or vice versa. But Tuesdays were always good. Tuesdays, Daniel didn't have to go to Co-Op if he didn't feel like it, and Erik didn't have to teach class until later, so they could Skype.

One Tuesday early in November, Daniel began his pre-Skype ritual. His ancient laptop was riddled with problems, including a disturbing aptitude for suddenly turning off for no particular reason. He re-taped his power cord firmly into place, a necessary step as his battery refused to hold a charge, and tried to find a spot with good lighting within the tethered reach of the wall socket.

Erik called him as soon as he was signed in, and, as usual, Daniel's laptop refused to cooperate. It would show frozen jittering video images, or would produce static-filled faintly garbled audio, but not both at the same time. Daniel sighed and turned off the video. It was much better to hear Erik than to see strange screencaps of his face.

"We need... get you... new computer," Erik's voice came through.

"Yes. Sorry." It was always easiest if Daniel spoke in short one-word bursts.

"I've... news... Monday."

"What about Sunday?"

"Monday."

"What about Monday, then?" Daniel laughed.

"Coming... things... do."

"Coming where?"

"There!" Daniel could hear a small spurt of Erik's laughter.

"Here? You're coming here?"

"Yes... next weekend... surprise... explain later."

"It's a surprise? For you?"

"You!"

"I love you." Daniel grinned at his computer.

"... Love you, too."

The call dropped then, and Erik began typing a message to him:

My flight arrives Monday morning. Can you be free this week? We've got things to do.

What kind of things? And yes, I don't have much going on during the week, and I'm sure I can take off work.

Monday, too, if you can.

What are we doing?

Mostly running around. But for a good cause. You'll like it, in the end, I think.

I feel like I should make some kind of snickering comment about usually always liking it in the end.

Always you with the dirty mind.

You like it. You love me and you know it.

Yes, I do. I have to go to the site soon. I switched teaching classes with Lars to get the time off.

Ooh, how's Thor doing?

Fine. He and Nikita are going out.

Nikita, huh?

Lars is very open-minded.

Also really, really hot.

Yes. But, no, we're not going to date him. I'll forward you the email with my flight details.

But you're not going to tell me what's going on?

No. I only get one chance telling you this and I want to see your face when I do.

Oh, my god, are you pregnant? Are we having a baby?

Ha ha so funny I forgot to laugh.

You're just bitter you haven't found someone to make an honest man out of you.

I did. He's you.

I love you.

I love you, too. I have to go, I'll talk to you soon.

📱

EVEN THOUGH DANIEL TRIED TO get it out of Erik via email, Erik refused to give him any insight into what was bringing him suddenly back to Tallenburg, or what they'd be doing all week.

Daniel tried to be cool, tried to be calm and collected, but a goofy grin burst on his face as soon as Erik came through the arrivals door with his bag slung over his shoulder.

Erik looked amused as he made his way through the slower-moving crowd.

"Now, are you going to tell me what you're doing here?"

"Not yet. Later." Erik kissed him as they waited for a taxi.

It was a long, torturous ride back to Daniel's apartment.

"LOOK, LET ME JUST SAY this," Daniel started as he knelt down on the rumpled sheets a few hours later. "Let's do this, now."

"Do what, now?" Erik chuckled and put one arm behind his head, stretching lazily. "I certainly can't do a lot right now. I'm not a teenager, anymore."

"Start our lives together. Let's just do it. Let's say the words out loud, so we both hear it and we both know it." Daniel's words tumbled out. "Let's just keep working toward feeling like we do, right now. I'm just so fucking in love with you right now, Erik. I just love you so much. And I don't ever want to doubt that again. I don't ever want to lose sight of that again."

"I love you, too." Erik's brown eyes sparkled as he softly traced patterns on Daniel's leg.

"I just, I realized something, when we were... not together. You and I, we're not two halves of a whole. We're a balance. We bring out the best in each other, and maybe the worst, too. When you're dark, I'm light. When you're serious, I'm not. When I'm angry or upset, you're calm. We keep each other in balance, and that's what, that's what I want to spend the rest of my life doing. I just want to say that out loud. I want to spend the rest of my life loving you. And fighting with you. And being annoyed with you. And laughing at your jokes. And making you smile." Daniel had to stop before his throat closed up.

"I want that, too," Erik said softly, pulling Daniel down to lay next to him. "No matter what, we're not giving up on each other. No matter what, we're not giving up on 'us.'"

"And we don't need to get engaged, or get married or do any of that stupid ridiculous stuff—"

"Well, maybe we could—" Erik kissed Daniel's forehead.

"No, really," Daniel protested. "We don't. I always thought that I wanted all of that, the huge white wedding, the big reception, a million people there. But what I really was dreaming of, all along, was just someone standing in front of me and promising to love me for the rest of my life, someone choosing *me*, someone who I loved more than I ever knew I could love someone. Someone saying he'd choose to be with me, just like I am, with all my good things and my bad things, and in sickness and in health and all that. It was never about having a dream wedding. It was about having someone say they were never going to leave, that we were in this together until the end. And maybe even after that."

"I promise. All those things." Erik kissed him, on the mouth, on his cheek, on his eyelids. "Through everything, through anything life will throw at us. You and me, we'll face it together."

"Then that's all I need. This is enough for me. *You* are what I always wanted."

Erik smiled, a mischievous grin. "But, if I asked you again, what would you say?"

"I would say 'yes.' Obviously." Daniel grinned back. "But with the stipulation that we never ever, ever, have to plan a huge, ridiculous wedding."

"I'd be okay with that," Erik said, kissing him again. "Danny, love of my life? Will you marry me?"

Daniel kissed him, long and slow and deep. "Yes. Will you marry me?"
"Yes."

DANIEL DIDN'T THINK ERIK MEANT to fall asleep after that. He really didn't. One minute, he was smiling as he listened to Daniel talk chatter about his renewed energy, about working on Mrs. Reinholt's windows and the challenges he was having. His face glowed just as it used to and he was so beautiful. Erik looked so goddamned happy that he just fell asleep.

Two hours later, Daniel gently shook him awake. The light coming through the windows was late-afternoon dim.

"Hey, sleepyhead?" Daniel said. "I'm sorry to wake you up, but I wasn't sure if you wanted to sleep right through, and stay on Sweden-time, or if you want to try to adjust?"

"No," Erik's voice was gravelly. "I want to adjust. We only have a couple of days together. I don't want to be asleep while you're awake. I'll miss too much. I'll get up."

Daniel smile was relieved, and happy. "Okay. I made some coffee, just in case."

"I'm sorry I fell asleep. I want to hear more about the windows and everything. You're incredible. And I love you."

"I love you, too." Daniel giggled. "Do you want me to bring you a cup in here, or—"

"No, no, I'll get up." He swung his legs over the side of the bed, scrubbing at his face with both hands. "Ugh. Jet lag."

"Ugh, jet lag, indeed." Daniel wrinkled up his nose. "Are you ready for some dinner, too?"

"Yeah," Erik interrupted himself with a huge jaw-cracking yawn. "Dinner would be great."

"I'll go start it."

Daniel ambled into the kitchen and turned on the gas under a pot of water. He'd bought fancy pasta at the fancy Italian store for the occasion:

tiny raviolis stuffed with truffles and cheese. *I'll make a simple white wine sauce*, he thought. Binge-watching the Cooking Network had really inspired him lately.

Erik shuffled into the kitchen. "Do you need any help?"

"No way am I letting you near any sharp implements or fire while you're still in a zombie daze. No, sir." Daniel waggled his head and put a cup of coffee down in front of him. "You sit there and drink this and look gorgeous."

Erik chuckled. His chair squeaked as he sat down and it wobbled slightly under him.

"Yeah," Daniel said, grabbing a sauté pan from the shelf. "That chair hasn't gotten any better since you've been gone."

Erik blew on his coffee, then took a sip. "We've got some things to discuss. Three things, actually."

"Oh?" Daniel sniffed as he sliced shallots for the sauce.

"So, here it is." Erik cleared his throat.

"Oh god. This doesn't sound good."

"No, it's fine. Really." Erik slurped more coffee. "It's just that I've sold my collection."

"You did what?" Daniel's mouth dropped open, but he kept his eyes trained on the shallot he was slicing.

"Actually, I put it up for auction."

"You did what?"

"Yeah, I had put it up for auction a couple of months ago, and the auction they scheduled was last week, and it generated quite a bit of interest."

"Quite a bit?"

"There was actually a bidding war."

"Oh, my god, seriously?" Daniel stopped slicing. "For your magazines about Vitophanic Tryptodarium?"

Erik's eyebrows creased lightly in confusion. "That's not in any of the stories."

"No, I just made it up, goofball." Daniel went back to slicing. "But, seriously, there was a bidding war? That's amazing!"

"Yes," Erik said. "Even I was surprised."

"Well, who won the auction?"

"A Mr. Hikaro Takahashi of Tokyo. Apparently, he's a huge fan of Timothy McMurphy."

"For how much?"

"Minus the auction house's fees." Erik paused, grinning. "Two point eight million dollars."

The knife clattered out of Daniel's hand as he spun around. "Shut up."

"No, really."

"Shut *up*!"

"I'm not joking." Erik laughed at the dumbstruck expression on Daniel's face.

"Shut the fuck up." Daniel burst out laughing. "Someone paid you two point eight million dollars for your collection of magazines?"

"Antique magazines in excellent-to-pristine condition, yes."

"Oh, my god."

"Yes." Erik nodded.

"I just can't believe you did that." Daniel was happily stunned. "I mean, you loved those magazines—"

"No." Erik yawned. "I mean, I loved *some* of them, and I have extra copies of the ones I really enjoyed. But once I decided to collect the whole thing, the idea always was to sell them off eventually."

"That's just—I just don't even know what to say." Daniel grinned. "Do we need to go pack them up, or something? Put all the boxes in boxes?"

"No, the auction house came already and packed them up, weeks and weeks ago. Antonio kind of supervised it for me." Erik poured more milk in his coffee, clattering the cup back on the table. "So, we need to discuss what we want to do."

"What *we* want to do with what?" Daniel picked up the knife and started slicing herbs.

"You're going to be my husband, Daniel. You have a say in what happens to this money."

Daniel smiled. *Husband.* "How the hell should I know? Buy a castle? With swans and a moat?"

"We could do that." Erik laughed. "If we wanted to."

"Oh, my god."

"I made an appointment with a financial advisor for tomorrow afternoon." Erik sipped more coffee. "I'm inclined to *not* buy a castle and instead invest most of the money."

"That sounds responsible. And adult." Daniel swiped everything into the sauté pan.

"Well, we'll meet with the advisor tomorrow and see what she has to say. I want us to be able to live comfortably for a very long time together."

"Oh, my god," Daniel said again, setting the timer for the pasta. "I just can't believe this."

"We've got papers to sign and accounts to set up and things to do."

"Why do I need to sign papers, again?"

Erik yawned. "Well, everything would be a lot less complicated if we really were married. All of the legal intricacies would be a lot more straightforward if you were my husband, not just my domestic life partner."

"Okay," Daniel said, stirring the pan.

"So, what do you think about getting married at City Hall tomorrow morning?"

"Oh, my god." Daniel laughed. "Okay, sure. Why not!"

"I feel bad. I feel like you're being cheated."

"How am I being cheated, marrying the man I love?"

"Because I'm bringing up all these non-romantic reasons, and you might think that that's the only reason, and not that it's really because I love you and want to be with you for the rest of our lives and want us to share everything."

"I know it's not the only reason, Erik." Daniel pushed Erik's chair back from the table and sat on his lap and kissed him. "It's perfect."

The chair creaked ominously. "This chair is a menace," Erik said between kisses.

"I know." Daniel got up carefully. "Wait, what was the third thing?"

"Ah, right." Erik cleared his throat again. "I've been offered a professorship at the University of Stockholm."

"Oh, wow!" Daniel grinned again. "Okay."

"I haven't accepted it yet. We need to make that decision together."

"I mean, of course you should take it!"

"It means moving there for at least a few years." Erik said carefully. "I—I don't want to be without you, Danny. We'd have to talk about how we'd handle flying back and forth."

"Or we could talk about how I could move there with you."

"But Co-Op, what would you do about that?"

"Internet sales are actually picking up, ever since Stasia found that photographer to barter yarn with. Things are kind of flying off the shelves already. So, I don't really *need* to be here in Tallenburg."

"There might be tax implications," Erik murmured. As usual, he began looking around for a piece of paper to take notes on. "And import/export, and—" He trailed off as Daniel handed him paper and pen.

Erik scribbled down things to ask the financial advisor as Daniel finished cooking dinner.

"You'll really move to Stockholm with me?" He asked almost wistfully when Daniel set the plates on the table.

"You're stuck with me, Kappel." Daniel teased.

"Good. That's exactly where I want to be."

THEY GOT TO CITY HALL around ten a.m. the next morning, with their hair still damp from their shower, in dress shirts and jeans. Standing on the front steps was Kate, beaming from ear-to-ear and holding two boutonnieres.

"What are you doing here?" Daniel shrieked as he and Erik climbed the stairs.

"I—I know I should have said something," Erik explained. "I wanted it to be a surprise. I emailed them when I set up my flights home, just on the off-chance my plan worked out the way I wanted it. Although, if you'd said no, you really didn't want to get married, I told them all I'd call off the plan."

"Told them all, who?" Daniel's voice was muffled because Kate was hugging him around his neck so tightly.

"I'm sorry I'm late, dears," a voice came from the bottom of the steps. It was Gloria.

"Here she is," Erik said happily, trotting back down the stairs toward her.

"Oh, my god!" Daniel giggled.

"Well, hello there to you, too," Gloria shouted as Erik held out his arm to help her up the stairs.

"Gloria!" Daniel yelped happily. He took her other arm when they reached him.

"Back when we were planning the, the first wedding, you said there were people you would really love to have standing up there with you, as a formal acknowledgment of how much you cared about them. You said it was really important to you," Erik explained as they climbed the rest of the steps.

"You remembered that?" Daniel whispered.

"It's the only time planning that wedding that you said something was really important to *you*."

"Oh, Erik." Daniel felt as though he might explode with happiness.

"I'm sorry Kate and Gloria were the only ones I could get ahold of—"

"Oh, my god," Daniel said. "It's perfect."

"Thankfully, Gloria here," Erik said as he smiled down at her, "agreed to stand up with me, as my best woman."

Gloria beamed first at Erik and then at Daniel. She pulled them close to her by tugging on their arms, so tiny between them their heads almost touched over her. "Oh, nothing could be better than being here with my two boys on their special day."

They couldn't keep smiles off their faces as they waited in line. Their hands shook so badly, Kate took the boutonnieres from them and pinned them on herself.

"We can't let you bleed all over on your wedding day," she scolded. "No gory wedding day photos, thank you very much."

The wedding license waiting period was quickly waived when they explained about Erik's international flights the next day. They waited in a small room lined with chairs filled with other beaming couples waiting to be married.

Their names were called. Erik's hand was icy as he held Daniel's which, he noted with amusement, had begun to sweat. As they made their way down the hallway, he whispered, "I'm so in love with you."

Daniel smiled at him, that special quiet glowing smile. "I'm so in love with you, too."

Epilogue

There is already an Aurora account associated with this e-mail address. Are you sure you would not like to restore your previous checklists?

📱

WELCOME BACK, DANIEL!

We're so happy to see you again! Thank you for choosing Aurora, the Ultimate Wedding Planning app!

You have chosen to create your own custom checklist: "Daniel and Erik Start Their Life Together/Goodbye Party Blowout Extravaganza."

You've got a lot of decisions to make and we've got a lot to help you with, so let's get cracking!

☑ *Send invitee list to party planner. (Click <u>here</u> for contact list.)*

☑ *Send check to party planner.*

☑ *Show up.*

📱

SIX MONTHS AFTER THEY GOT married, Daniel and Erik were finally living on the same continent. Daniel had finished the windows at the Reinholt house and had worked out a plan with the rest of Co-Op. He wasn't so sure how well it was going to work, but it was something to start with, at least.

He arrived in Stockholm one bright evening in May, with two large, bulging suitcases and an over-full carry-on bag. Erik grinned as he caught him in a giant hug. They stumbled getting the bags onto the train to their new apartment.

They'd bought their place on Daniel's last trip to Sweden: a loft on the outskirts of Stockholm in an up-and-coming neighborhood. Their block was full of newer shops and start-ups: a candy shop selling retro-styled candies, an organic specialty meatball shop. Daniel thought maybe something like Co-Op would fit right in, someday.

The loft had bleached wood floors, tall ceilings and walls painted white. They didn't have much in the way of furniture, but they weren't sure if they really needed much. Scandinavian style, as Daniel was finding, was about having space and being uncluttered. He liked it very much.

Erik dragged Daniel's suitcases up the stairs and into the loft. "Shut up and don't argue, love. You're jetlagged and exhausted and you breaking your neck on the stairs on our first day together isn't in the plan."

Erik had moved in last month; most of his things were still in boxes and crates. "It didn't seem right to set anything up without you here."

Daniel shuffled all the way to the far corner of the loft, to the area in which Erik had set up their bed. He made Erik laugh by dramatically flopping on the bed, face-first. "Bed. Now." He moaned with his face half-buried in the duvet. "Please. You. Me. Sleep."

"You're ridiculous." Erik chuckled and lay down next to him, rubbing his back. "You'll probably do better if you sleep through tonight and start getting on schedule tomorrow."

"Do we have anything going on tomorrow? Anything important?" Daniel asked, plaintively. "Anything we *have* to do?"

"Just getting on with the rest of our lives," Erik smiled.

Daniel flung one arm over his husband, pulling him close and kissed him. "The rest of our lives sounds very good to me."

FIN

Acknowledgments

THIS BOOK HAS TAKEN QUITE a journey to the printed page, and as such I have a great many people to thank for helping me along the way

Lex, for everything.

My wonderful team at Interlude Press, for their dedication and support. To my editor, Annie, for being such a guiding light; to Candy for her perseverance and hard work; and to the ever-incredible CB Messer for knowing exactly what I meant when I told her what I'd envisioned for the cover.

Carrie and Brew for their love and steadfast support, for being the sassiest, most fun people I know.

Lissa, for slogging through the very first drafts of this book, for making my brain sparkle and for being my friend.

The rest of my IP family – I appreciate and adore you guys more than I can say. This has been such a rough year for a lot of us, and I've been so grateful for your support. I know I'm going to forget to add someone, but especial thanks to Jude Sierra for her heart and the world's greatest double-take hug and to Lynn Charles for being so wonderful I can't pick out just a few things to thank her for. Alysia Constantine and Charlotte Ashe probably didn't know they were helping me sand down the rough edges of this book while we were road-tripping through Amish country, but I was taking it all in and I thank them for that, and for being such glorious blasts of color in my head. To Laura Stone for being articulate, savvy and fabulous, also for missing him as much as I do.

And finally, this book could not have been written without the love and support of my family, who are the light of my life. Thank you.

About the Author

K. E. BELLEDONNE IS A writer, editor and translator. A native New Englander, Kat spends her spare time listening to Glenn Miller records, reading history books and cheering on her beloved Red Sox. Her first novel, *Right Here Waiting*, was published by Interlude Press in 2015.

One **story**
can change **everything.**

@interlude**press**

Twitter | Facebook | Instagram | Pinterest

For a reader's guide to
Daniel & Erik's Super Fab Ultimate Wedding Checklist
and book club prompts, please visit interludepress.com.

also by
k.e. **belledonne**

In 1942, Ben Williams had it all—a fulfilling job, adoring friends and the love of his life, Pete Montgomery. But World War II looms over them. When Pete follows his conscience and joins the Army Air Force as a bomber pilot, Ben must find the strength to stay behind without his lover, the dedication to stay true and the courage he never knew he'd need to discover his own place in the war effort.

ISBN (print) 978-1-941530-22-1 | ISBN (eBook) 978-1-941530-28-3

Burning Tracks by Lilah Suzanne

In the sequel to Broken Records, Gwen Pasternak seems to have it all: a job she loves as stylist to the stars and a beautiful wife, Flora, by her side. But as her excitement in working alongside country music superstar Clementine Campbell grows, Gwen starts to second-guess the quiet domesticity she has waiting at home. Meanwhile, her business partner, Nico Takahashi and his partner, reformed bad-boy musician Grady Dawson, face future-based uncertainties of their own.

ISBN (print) 978-1-941530-99-3 | ISBN (eBook) 978-1-945053-00-9

Into the Blue by Pene Henson

Tai Talagi and Ollie Birkstrom have been inseparable since they met as kids surfing the North Shore. Now they live with their best friends in a pulled-together family, sharing life and the saltwater in their veins. Tai's spent years setting aside his feelings for Ollie, but when Ollie's pro surfing aspirations come to fruition, their steady world shifts. Is the relationship worth risking everything for a chance at something terrifying and beautiful and altogether new?

ISBN (print) 978-1-941530-84-9 | ISBN (eBook) 978-1-941530-85-6

The Rules of Ever After by Killian B. Brewer
Published by Duet, an imprint of Interlude Press

The royal rules have governed the kingdoms of Clarameer for centuries, but princes Phillip and Daniel know that these rules don't apply to them. In a quest to find their own Happily Ever After, they encounter meddlesome fairies, an ambitious stepmother, disgruntled princesses and vengeful kings as they learn about life, love, friendship and family—and learn to write their own rules of ever after.

ISBN (print) 978-1-941530-35-1 | ISBN (eBook) 978-1-941530-42-9